Grave Undertakings

Suzi Quatro

NEW HAVEN PUBLISHING LTD

Published 2025
First Edition
New Haven Publishing Ltd
www.newhavenpublishingltd.com
newhavenpublishing@gmail.com

Cover design©Pete Cunliffe

new haven

Prologue

This book idea was born approximately forty years ago and that's just a guess. It has been on the back burner of my mind and finally it's time to take it out of the oven. Maybe living through the pandemic has something to do with it. Who knows?

It is the eternal question, is it not… How would we all like to be remembered?

I travelled the length and breadth of people's psyches to obtain the collection of tombstone inscriptions at the end of this book. Some told a joke, some sang a song, some were sombre, some were touching, and some philosophical. Some have met their maker after giving me their quotes, and I hope I have done them justice.

I have left no stone unturned (pun intended).

You are born alone, and you die alone, and that for me says it all. I remember stopping at a gas station years ago while touring America and seeing a sign on the wall that read:

"Please, don't let me get to the end of my life, and find out I haven't lived!"

That's how I feel about it. You have to LIVE life for all it's worth. You must embrace, dance, scream, cry, dream, laugh, struggle, hurt, and love, every single minute of every single day.

I have asked this question to various people, and most do not agree with me at all, but a few of them have. I would like to know exactly when my time will be up this side of life, to the exact second. "WHY?" I can hear you shouting. Because I don't want to be late! And that's my personal little quirk.

What I thought was going to be just quotes and illustrations on tombstones, quite unexpectedly turned into an actual novel.

Enjoy my story, as Penelope Perfect and Max Morose, and a few others, take us through a course in psychology and the meaning of life and death and everything in between.
Now before I begin, here is my tombstone inscription.

I get a double sided one because I am a Gemini, and because it's MY book!

WATCH YOUR STEP!
SUZI QUATRO, JUNE 3 1950, DETROIT MICHIGAN

1."NOW I GET IT!"

2."TOO MANY DREAMS, TOO LITTLE TIME"

Let the Class Begin

Miss Penelope Perfect lived a very quiet, comfortable life in a very quiet suburb of Chicago. She was from a large family of six kids, two sisters and three brothers, and although she loved escaping into the city sometimes, just to find some space, she really preferred to spend her young life at home, safe and secure, as noisy as it was. Her childhood years passed quietly without much drama or excitement. She had a few boyfriends here and there, but nothing serious. And being from such a large family meant there was no need for outside circles of friends: she had it all indoors.

Penelope was a pretty good student and was extremely interested in psychology from her early teens. Hidden inside her was a sharp, curious mind, in direct contrast with the soft-spoken, sweet looking young lady she had turned into, and, after graduating high school, she found herself at Harvard University, studying to be a psychologist. It was at the first lecture she noticed 'him 'on the other side of the classroom. It was her first experience of such a deep reaction to the opposite sex and she was not at all sure how to handle it. This was uncharted waters, and she wasn't sure if she wanted to swim or not.

Mr. Max Morose was an only child, raised by his divorced mother and grandmother. He grew up in Brooklyn, not poor, but very close to it. They lived in a tiny apartment, freezing in the winter and boiling in the summer, one bathroom shared with four other tenants, a tiny kitchen, two and a half bedrooms, dining nook, and an outside fire escape his mother liked to refer to as their balcony. He always had enough to eat, and he always had enough love; in fact, too much love, especially from his mother, who had thought that at the age of thirty-eight her chances of having a baby were nil. She made him the most important thing in her life, which had good and bad results in the man he would turn out to be.

He had ambition, because that was all he could afford to have. From a very young age he was determined to be a success. He dreamed and schemed from the time he could think for himself. Money and power - this is what motivated Max; money and power equalled freedom, and although he leaned towards negativity, his motivation was positive enough. "Bring it on, universe; I'm ready for the ride!"

He was also, like Penelope, a good student at school, and gravitated towards subjects of the mind but with the added string to his bow of being a talented cartoonist. He was not sure which career to pursue. He considered himself a tough cookie, not easy to fool, a 'no bullshit 'kind of character. After considering various options for his further education, he became the recipient of a scholarship to go to Harvard and study psychology. Should he or shouldn't he... and since he could not think of a good reason to turn it down, he moved out of his apartment in Brooklyn, waved a tearful goodbye to the woman who worshipped him, hugged his grandmother and moved into the dormitory at Harvard, ready and more than willing to discover what the world had in store for him.

The alarm went off at 7:30 a.m., day one for Penelope. A little nervous, she got dressed, low key, so as not to attract too much attention, grabbed her schedule, her rucksack and her comb, and headed to the first class of the day.

8:00 a.m. the alarm went off in Max Morose's bedroom. He quickly showered, put on his favourite pair of jeans, t-shirt, denim jacket, and being a big fan of the old classic movies like *On the Waterfront* starring Marlon Brando, he said out loud, "I coulda been a contender!" and made his way to his first class of the day at Harvard University, whistling softly down the hallowed halls of ivy.

Professor Handover was the teacher of this course in psychology and human behaviour. It was an unusual class, made up of only a handful of students; six, to be exact, more like a tutorial. He was of Austrian descent, rather stern but nice looking, fifty years old, going a little thin on top, with a penchant for pinstriped suits with a carnation in the buttonhole and a white pocket square folded into a triangle sticking out of his top pocket, topped off with a white shirt and a pink tie. This pink tie was his only form of rebellion. And, of course, to complete the picture, he wore rubber soled shoes so no one would hear him coming!

The class of six filed in hesitantly, quiet and a little curious, as no one knew each other, finding seats and sitting down. Penelope and Max took the two seats at either end of the semi-circle. They were both observers of humanity and had a view of the entire 'stage', as it were. Just the way they both liked it. Unnoticed until they chose to be noticed.

Professor Handover stood up from the chair behind his desk, strode around to the front facing his pupils, clearing his throat rather deliberately, and said, "Good morning, students, welcome to the first day of the rest of your life - philosophically speaking, of course!"

Class 1

"Now then, young ladies and young gentleman, may I welcome you to my class." He paused for a long beat, looking slowly round the semi-circle, taking in every student.

He finally continued:

"During this course we will be dissecting human emotion, and instinct, and how they play out in our lives, and indeed our inevitable deaths. How do you feel about life, in general, what is its purpose, is there a God, are you afraid to live fully in case there are consequences, are you afraid to die in case there is a hell, and you have not qualified for the other place… is it better, or indeed easier, to be an optimist, or is it best to be a pessimist? Let's start with a little experiment to get us going." Looking slowly again around the room, Professor Handover pointed to a good-looking young man slouching in his chair, half gazing out the window.

"You... what is your name?"

A little startled but immediately alert, the young man replied, "Peter Pendergast, sir," sitting up a little straighter.

"Well, Peter… Are you an optimist or a pessimist?"

"Well, sir, I believe I am an optimist. I tend towards the 'every cloud has a silver lining'… but sir… I do have a pessimistic friend. In fact, he is so low, when they bury him, they're going to have to dig up!"

The class politely tittered, not sure if this was an appropriate time for a joke, funny though it was.

Professor Handover smiled, just a teeny bit, and just for a second. (File him under 'class clown.')

He pointed again, to the other side of the room, this time to a young woman, alluringly dressed in skinny black jeans, high heels, plain black t-shirt, and a black French beret perched on her head, with flowing black hair hanging halfway down her back, and two large, silver, dangling hooped earrings.

"Hello, Professor. My name is Lillie Lawford, and I am a pessimist.

"I follow the line of thought that for every good, there is a bad, and if I have to cast a vote, it goes to the bad side every time. Then you're not being constantly disappointed."

This brought a look of interest to the Professor's face, again, briefly. (File her under 'darkly exotic and attractive.') Then he focused back on the job at hand. He was aware that this, in its own way, was not only his introduction to his students, but their introduction to each other, and therefore everyone was wearing their Sunday best, intellectually speaking of course.

Slowly making his way around the room again, he settled on another young man, who was staring studiously at him. This one was wearing thick glasses, and had mousey brown cropped hair, a grey v-neck sweater, a white shirt, a tie, baggy trousers and penny loafers, which made him look a step out of time.

"You," looking directly at him, "what's your name please?"

"Mr. Edmund P. Woodhouse Jr. sir," he replied in a thin, high, squeaky voice. "And I believe I am an optimist, most of the time, although I do have my darker moments, in fact strictly speaking I could be swayed either way but I do lean towards the positive. We often have this kind of discussion over the dinner table, which is always informative and interesting, kind of like a Greek debate about the wheres and whyfors of life. My father often says that…"

"Thank you, Edmund," the professor said, abruptly putting a stop to Edmund's monologue. "We get the picture." (File him under 'nerd'.) "Well, let's hope this course helps you decide which indeed you are, because most of us are either glass half full or glass half empty people." Eyes roaming round again, he settled on another young woman. This one was tall, angular, bobbed brown hair, intelligent, challenging eyes, and slightly sad looking, but pleasant with it.

"You, young lady, please introduce yourself."

"Hello Professor, my name is Patricia Hodges, and I am most definitely, non-negotiable, a pessimist. As much as I would like to believe in a knight in shining armour, galloping along and rescuing me and having a fairy tale, everybody-lives-happily-ever-after ending… I just can't believe in it," and realising she'd said a little too much, and been way too personal, she stopped right there, casting her eyes back down to her pad and pencil sitting on the desk. She slowly lowered her tall frame back onto the seat.

Hmm, Professor Handover thought. Very interesting indeed, there's a story there to be told or I'll eat my hat. (File her under 'wounded'.)

"Okay, you, young lady."

Penelope looked up hesitantly.

"Yes sir, hello Professor, hello everybody. My name is Penelope Perfect, although I can assure you, I am not." She giggled lightly, letting a genuine smile play across her cute features as her eyes swept the room. "I can say without a doubt I am an optimist. I have been this way my entire life, much to the dismay of my siblings. They say I look at everything through rose-coloured glasses, and that I am unrealistic. Well, if seeing beauty instead of ugliness, hope instead of despair, love instead of hate, makes me unrealistic, then hallelujah." Then, reciting in rhythm, tapping her foot to her internal beat, she said:

"Unrealistic I will stay,
 Optimistic all the way,
 And that's my poem for the day."

A small spattering of applause. Which both pleased Penelope and made her blush, which made her look even more charming.

Professor Handover looked Penelope directly in the eye, a little longer than he had anyone else. She met his gaze, showing both strength and vulnerability in equal measures.

"And finally, you sir, far right, in the denim ensemble… what is your name?"

"Hello to you sir, I am Max Morose, and possibly one of the most certified hard cases of pessimism you will ever encounter. Always have been. I don't have any siblings with which to argue the toss, in fact nobody but my mother and grandmother. I have not been born with a silver spoon in my mouth, plastic would be more accurate. I am here on a scholarship, and happy to be so. But this course is a means to an end. It is something I am good at, dissecting the human mind, but I gotta tell you Professor… ain't nothing gonna change MY attitude." Max directed this last gem of wisdom at Penelope. For a brief moment their eyes locked, really locked. Chalk and cheese had met, and their dance began from this moment on.

Professor Handover caught the entire exchange… very interesting. (File him under 'deep, or deep under'.) Chuckling to himself, the professor looked forward to seeing this relationship develop.

Clearing his throat, he stood up very tall, making it obvious that the first session was over.

"Alright class, welcome to each one of you. This was more of a saying hello to each other rather than a full-blown lesson. Your assignment for next week is to do some research. There is an excellent library on campus. I would like you all to come up with two famous figures from history, and illustrate, using their own words, which you think they are, pessimist or optimist.

"See you next week."

The class filed out, each deep in their own thoughts. There were a few tentative "hello"s and "hi"s here and there, but no real conversation. Not yet. It was all too new for everyone.

Penelope slowly made her way out of the building, observing college life, students scurrying down the hallway, lockers being shut, doors closing, a symphony of students chit chatting away, and finally out the exit, which turned into well-manicured, winding pathways. Well, here I am, she said to herself, here I am. I think I will begin my research today. Glancing up, she saw several signs with arrows pointing in various directions. There we go:' Library', to the left.

Max slouched, looking moody, as was his way, and meandered down the hallway, not in any hurry, looking neither left nor right, simply sensing the exit doors.

So, this is it. Here I am; God, I hope I made the right choice, he thought to himself; well, at least there is one interesting person in the class… that Penelope. She is so cute, cute and intelligent, now there's a bonus for you! The professor is no slouch either.

Methinks he sizes people up quickly and accurately. Have to watch myself with that one. Right, off I go to the library.

The other four, Peter, Lillie, Edmund and Patricia, all decided to go back to their separate lodgings, and make a fresh start in the morning.

Penelope found the library without any problem. It was beautiful and peaceful. She loved libraries, always had: you can be surrounded by people, yet totally lose yourself. So quiet. Heaven. Being from such a big family had left her with a permanent need for silence, golden or not.

Sitting down, she took out her notepad and began to make some notes. Now... let's think of some historic figures that I find interesting. Okay, politics, Winston Churchill, he was known for making witty remarks; oh I know, one of my favourite books of all time, *The Prophet* by Khalil Gibran. He is bound to be illuminating!

She made her way to the various alphabetically listed biographies, grabbing down the ones she needed, then made her way back to the table.

It took a little time, nearly three hours, scanning each book, looking at reference notes and chapter sections, but eventually she was able to extract what she needed from her chosen two people's books. It was nearly 10:30 p.m., and by this time, she was mentally and physically exhausted. And so to bed!

Max was sitting, as he had in the classroom, at the other end of the library, having no idea Penelope was there; not that it would have made a difference. It was not time yet to start up a conversation. He needed to observe her a little more before he made his move. He saw she was naturally shy and knew that indeed he would have to make the first move. He sat there thinking. Okay, I want two people who are edgy and will impress the professor. Let's see now, who impresses me? Friedrich Nietzsche. Excellent choice, Max boy. And Socrates; I mean, talk about a philosopher. He then proceeded to N and S, extracted the books, and read them through until he found what he needed. And then for him too, it was sleep time... into the arms of Morpheus.

The week passed slowly for all the new students, which was fine, as they all had a brand-new domain to discover.

Class 2

Monday morning, 9:00 a.m., Professor Handover's class filled up once again. The students took the same seats they had sat in the first time. He waited for everyone to settle and quieten down, cleared his throat out of habit rather than need, and began.

"Right, let's begin. First up, Peter. Would you like to share with the class your two historical figures and their quotations, please?"

Peter picked up his notebook from the desk, stood, and addressed the room.

"Yes, sir. First, I picked the great American writer Mark Twain. He had this to say: 'I didn't attend the funeral, but I sent a nice letter saying I approve of it.'

"And second, Oscar Wilde, who said, 'Biography lends to death a new terror.' I believe his last words were 'Either the curtains go, or I do', and then he died. A very quotable man. Both Twain and Wilde are very humorous, don't you think?"

"Very good, Peter, thank you. Now over to you Lillie, can we have your two, please?"

Lillie flung her long dark hair over her shoulder just for the effect, and slowly rose to face the room, pausing dramatically. Plucking the retro shaped pink sunglasses from her blouse and chewing on one of the arms, she began.

"I have chosen first, Benjamin Franklin, who said, 'Some people die at 25 and aren't buried until 75.' Love that.

"And second, the great poet, T. S. Eliot. 'I have seen birth and death but had thought they were different'."

"Very good Lillie, very good indeed. Next up, Mr. Woodhouse."

Edmund stood up almost to attention, looking very formal indeed, a direct product of his strict upbringing. Wiping his glasses to see better, he looked at his notes and began.

"Yes sir, Professor Handover, I thought long and hard about this, and went through many choices before I could finally settle, but I feel I have picked wisely, and I think, interestingly. Ahem... First I have chosen Helen Keller, who I have always found to be an amazing inspiration, having overcome being born deaf, dumb and blind. She said the following: 'Death is no more than passing from one room to another. But there is a difference for me, you know. Because in that other room, I shall be able to see'." There followed a natural silence as the class took that one in. "And second, Robert Green Ingersoll, who says, 'In the night of death, hope sees a star and listening love can hear the rustle of a wind'." Another silence followed.

"Thank you, Edmund, very unusual choices." (File that under 'surprising'.)

"Okay Patricia, you're up next. Let's see what an unshakable pessimist has chosen..."

Patricia rose and rose. She was 6 '1" tall, and was proud with it.

"Yes Professor, I too had many possibilities, but strived to get the exact ones to illustrate my own views... so, first up, Martin Luther King Jr. He says, 'If a man has not discovered something that he will die for, he isn't fit to live.' And second, Napoleon Bonaparte. 'Death is nothing, but to live defeated and inglorious is to die daily'." She immediately folded her lanky frame back into the chair.

"And now our final two. Miss Perfect. Off you go."

"Good morning, everyone, good morning, Professor. My choices. In my opinion one of the greatest politicians of all time, and always quotable, Winston Churchill, who said, 'I am prepared to meet my maker; whether he is prepared for the great ordeal of meeting me is another matter.'

"And second, one of my all-time favourite books is *The Prophet*, so I chose the author, Kahlil Gibran: 'Death most resembles a prophet who is without honour in his own land or a poet who is a stranger to his people'."

"And finally, Mr. Morose, enlighten us of your choices, if you would please."

Max stood moodily up, with that rebellious air that he'd had down pat since his teens. Smirking rather than smiling, he began, "Okay Professor, first up is Friedrich Nietzsche. 'The kingdom of heaven is a condition of the heart, not something that comes upon the earth or after death.'

"And second, Socrates, who says, 'Ordinary people seem not to realise that those who really apply themselves in the right way to philosophy are directly and of their own accord preparing for dying and death'."

Max proudly sat back down. He knew he had aced it with his choices.

"Thank you, everyone, and now we shall begin the business of dissecting these quotes."

Professor Handover was now in his element. Oh how he loved debate, dissection, digging into people's psyches; this was the reason why he chose his profession. The brain just fascinates me, he thought quietly to himself, while outwardly taking charge of the classroom with his stern demeanour, allowing a piece of his intellectual charisma to leak out. He began to teach.

"Now class, you are all at the very beginning of this course, and there is much to learn, and may I add, much to unlearn too. Never ever judge a book by its cover, including your own. Psychology is fascinating in every way, and eventually, hopefully, you will find yourself addicted to the discovery of how our brains work.

"Let's start with your chosen quotes, Peter. You chose Mark Twain and Oscar Wilde, both known for their wry humour and sarcasm. You have already declared that you are an optimist, therefore one can assume you chose these two writers because you feel their comments made them optimistic too. Am I correct in my assumption?"

"Yes, you are, Professor, a hundred per cent. It shows wit and humour, but also acceptance of the inevitable which comes to us all."

"And Peter, do you think these two chosen people are optimists, as you say you are?"

"Definitely, sir."

"How about we look at these quotes from another angle. How about Mark Twain's? 'I didn't attend the funeral but I sent a nice letter saying I approve of it.' Maybe this quote was born in a dark place, maybe this was him poking fun and ridicule at the entire idea of funerals and the rituals that follow, in a way negating the entire process, maybe deep down he was a pessimist, and covered this up with light, witty repartee… and look at Oscar Wilde's comment - known for his way with words and irony and sarcasm - 'Either the curtains go or I do.' Could he have been a closet pessimist? A depressed, frightened, lonely man, simply covering his passing with a typical Oscar Wilde remark, only to dissuade people from looking too closely at his broken heart, his broken mind, his broken life?"

This caused a long pause in the classroom, putting the students deep in thought. Peter was silent too and remained standing, obviously thinking about what he would reply, finally saying, "I'm sorry but I don't have an answer for you, I need to digest." He sat down, not making a sound.

"Excellent response, Peter, excellent. Methinks you are not just the class clown after all. That there is a deeply analytical mind in amongst all your light heartedness, and I have just possibly shaken a little of your foundations. Good. Enjoy your digestion. We may address these questions again later in the course.

"Okay. Next, our exotic pessimist, Lillie. Let's look at yours, shall we? First of all, have you chosen because you believe both Benjamin Franklin and T.S. Eliot were wired the same as you? Or did you choose them because you simply like what they had to say?"

Lillie was not caught off guard. She prided herself on always being one step ahead and had her responses and reasons ready for close inspection and dissection. Bring it on, she thought to herself, crossing her long legs, and planting a smug expression on her unusually attractive face.

"In my opinion, both quotes are born from negativity, which can be translated as pessimism or realism, depending on your point of view.

"Benjamin Franklin. Just love this one. Some people die at 25 but aren't buried until 75. This to me illustrates a man who does not suffer fools gladly, and sees the world exactly as it is. A lot of lost people, wandering around, helplessly stumbling to their end having achieved nothing. We see eye to eye, old Benjie and me... and T.S. Eliot, how clever and totally on the money is he? 'I have seen birth and death but thought they were different.' Now if both these are not perfect examples of pessimism, well then, I will eat my hat," she said, removing her French beret from her head, taking a dramatic bow side to side, and taking her seat with attitude. She had been clever, and she knew it.

Professor Handover gave her a penetrating stare, an uncomfortably long one, as he prepared his reply to this very bright, edgy and yes, very attractive, student.

"Okay Miss Lillie, you make a good point. I agree both comments seem to be pessimistic at first glance but let's twist their words, just for argument's sake. Maybe Benjamin Franklin was the eternal optimist, wanting his fellow man to wake up and smell the roses, but was frustrated in his quest repeatedly, and this was simply his way of trying to give humans a wakeup call. Maybe he was an angel of communication, hoping for the best possible outcome in the worst possible circumstance, which we call the 'human race'. Maybe he just 'got it', and was trying to spread the good word.

"And T.S. Eliot, maybe this is neither black nor white, but somewhere in between. Maybe his comment is reality without the rose-coloured glasses. Not a bad thing. Don't be so sure of your judgement of these two colourful, intelligent people. And Miss Lillie. Well done. Very well done.

"Next up, over to you, Mr. Edmund Woodhouse."

Edmund stood immediately and, as was his way, in a military fashion, with his pad and pen, ready, willing and able.

"Tell me something, Edmund, were you ever called anything else as a child, a nickname, something less formal? Just curious."

"No sir, it's only ever been Edmund. I come from a very proper family, you know. Were you aware that my family actually eats on genuine plates from Napoleon Bonaparte's personal collection?" He coughed. "But I digress. Here are my two choices. First, Helen Keller, whose story always inspires me to never give up; her quote is 'Death is no more than passing from one room to another. But there is a difference for me you know. In that other room I shall be able to see.' Isn't that an amazing quote? Wow. And my second choice, Robert Green Ingersoll, 'In the night of death, hope sees a star and listening love can hear a rustle of the winds.' Now that one blows me away." He chuckled. "Get it? Wind blows me away."

Making a joke was so out of character for Edmund that he turned bright red and quickly sat back down.

"Okay Edmund, and tell me, are these quotes optimistic or pessimistic in your opinion?"

"Helen Keller, easy. I would say she was the most optimistic person that ever existed, to even believe in a world that held no light, no sound, nothing. And Ingersoll, seems to me like he must have been a hopeless romantic, which of course is optimistic."

"I would agree with you Edmund, but would add that Helen Keller had to overcome her innate pessimism, which could also be called frustration, hence the fits, the rages, the screaming, to become the optimist she became. There is no arguing this point. She was a true optimist, and thank goodness, this was her ticket for survival. Let's take Ingersoll. I would say he was not realistic at all, even facing the Grim Reaper with hope in his heart as the sword cuts him down. Quite sweet in a way. Funny though, Helen Keller's optimism was a show of strength while Ingersoll's, I believe, is a show of weakness. I am leaning towards your opinion though, and thank you for the little joke, it was most amusing."

Clapping his hands together, getting into his stride, the professor swung his glance around the room, settling on the lofty Patricia Hodges.

"Ms. Hodges, can you enlighten us with your quotes please?"

Patricia rose a little hesitantly in her plaid skirt and matching cardigan, bobbed brown hair curled around her face, uncomfortable with all eyes on her, which gave her a unique, vulnerable charm, and began, "Okay, Martin Luther King, 'If a man has not discovered something he would die for, he isn't fit to live.' And my second choice, Napoleon Bonaparte, 'Death is nothing, but to live defeated and inglorious is to die daily.' I believe both quotes to be pessimistic."

"Now, Patricia, interesting. You have picked Martin Luther King, one of the most inspirational, fighting-for-equality speakers of our time, and Napoleon, one of the most successful wartime generals in time. In fact, both were fighters on different fields. I am curious as to why you think these quotes are pessimistic."

"Well sir, I would agree that on the face of it, especially with Martin Luther King, you would say he optimistically fought the good fight, fought for what he believed in. But I am looking deeper. I think that inside he was very pessimistic, and his 'dream' was just that: his dream, never to be realised in his lifetime, and which he did indeed die for or because of. Either way he is gone. I think his quote was a prediction from deep inside. He fought but did not win. And Napoleon, well, he kind of said the same thing in a more old-fashioned way. He was a little power crazy, and therefore judged himself on his wins... don't mention Waterloo!

"Neither of them was typical. I believe inside they were pessimists."

"Now, Patricia, you have given me food for thought. Interesting points you have made. I will ponder your opinions, and get back to you with my opinion, if I can come up with some counter arguments. Right... now, over to you, Miss Perfect; hmm, I like being able to call you this, Miss Perfect." He chuckled. "Let's have your two quotes please... and I am sure they will be perfectly perfect!"

God, I wish I had a different name, thought Penelope. "Well, Professor, my first choice is Winston Churchill, in my opinion one of the great politicians in history, he said, 'I am prepared to meet my maker, whether he is prepared for the great ordeal of meeting me is another matter.' Second, Kahlil Gibran, who I absolutely adore, you can take his book, *The Prophet*, and literally open it at any page and find something inspiring, thought provoking and beautiful. What a wonderful book this is. His quote is 'Death most resembles a prophet who is without honour in his own land or a poet who is a stranger to his people'."

"And Miss Perfect, do you find these quotes to be optimistic or pessimistic?"

"Well, Winston Churchill was known for his quick repartee; one of my favourites, and I am paraphrasing, is a lady came up to him at a party and said 'You are drunk sir,' to which he replied, 'And you, my dear, are ugly, and in the morning, I will be sober.' Or words to that effect. Although rude, you can't deny it's funny, at least to me. It's my sense of humour. I wouldn't want to verbally tangle with him. And another one, describing America and England, 'two nations divided by a common language.' Excellent. And speaking of Americans, by the way, Churchill's mother was American... and apparently Tallulah Bankhead was a friend of his too... hmm, which makes me think. I love Tallulah too. Maybe I will find a quote from her for next week's class. She was totally unique. Anyway, back to Mr. Churchill... I would say, yes, he was an optimist, and at the same time a realist, because he saw himself exactly as he was. I believe he followed my personal eleventh commandment: thou shalt not bullshit thyself. Excuse my French. He knew he was not an easy man. So that puts him ahead of the game immediately, and almost everyone else on the back foot. Good example to live by. Keep everyone just a little off centre. Now to Kahlil Gibran. I must admit I found this one to be a little confusing. He was this uneducated, wonderful prophet whose books have been translated into many languages, speaking truths, weaving words, teaching lessons many of us cannot learn in a lifetime... so his quote? Well, to me it borders on pessimism. What he is saying is, you MUST be honourable, and you MUST be known! The jury is still out on this one."

Then, stopping to take a breath, she added: "I am sorry, Professor Handover; it seems I did a little monologue without realising it... just got carried away."

"Yes, you did, Penelope, and you did it perfectly. There is more to you than meets the eye. Let's examine further. Mr. Churchill was indeed known for his wit, but he was also known for his uncompromising views, including religion and obviously politics. An optimistic quote, yes, I would say so, and with more than a touch of ego or confidence, whichever you like to call it, which is not a bad thing. Now, Kahlil Gibran, who I also adore. This is interesting indeed. In fact, let's go to the jury, and take a vote on it. Okay everyone… Gibran states that you must be honoured and known, which means he is speaking from an ego motivated place, which is surprising reading his books, which are totally selfless. Can we have a show of hands? Optimist first." Two hands were raised. "And now pessimist…" The remaining four hands went up. "Right. Pessimism wins. You, Max. You are up next anyway. Why do you personally think Kahlil Gibran's quote is on the negative side?"

Max stood up, pulling his nicely shaped mouth into a smug expression, his notes ready, and replied, "I don't think anyone can be as good and peaceful, inside and out, as Mr. Gibran appears to be. It kind of reminds me of the Japanese, always bowing so respectfully to everyone; nobody is that nice and polite all the time. I think Mr. Gibran's philosophy covered a very dark side of his inner psyche, a side he strove to hide, and therefore put the worth of his life into what he achieved with regards to honour and fame. And, if I was to have a dinner party, I would invite him for sure, along with Jesus, and my choices. Which I will share with you in a minute. Can I say, Miss Perfect, excellent quotes and interesting insights."

Max took a beat, and stared straight at Penelope, who stared straight back, freezing the moment forever in both of their hearts. Breaking the connection, he turned his gaze back to the teacher.

"So… Friedrich Nietzsche, one of the greatest minds of all time, and so very dark. 'The kingdom of heaven is a condition of the heart, not something that comes upon the earth or after death.' My second choice. Socrates. 'Ordinary people seem not to realise that those who really apply themselves in the right way to philosophy are directly and of their accord preparing for dying and death.'

"Now, Nietzsche, well, there is no doubt that he was completely pessimistic. He had very little faith in human nature - benefit of the doubt was not in his vocabulary - so his quote is basically saying, as his writing did, we are all living in a fantasy. And only in our hearts can we actually achieve heaven because in reality it does not exist, which opens up a real can of worms, if we want to go there… and the great philosopher Socrates, great and as deep as he was, and an inspiration to this day, he was pessimistically saying, 'to those of you with a brain, who can actually think it through, we are all going to die… end of.' Thank you."

Max, knowing he had been impressive, took a moment to look around the room, as if he was waiting for applause. When none came, he sat with an arrogant thump.

"Thank you, Max. Interesting quotes, and interesting opinions. I would say you can identify with both. I don't think *you* believe much in human nature, and I also think you put your brain above most people in this world. Now don't get me wrong, I am not picking on or insulting you whatsoever. It takes all kinds to make the world go round, but you are a hard nut to crack, you feel how you feel, you believe what you believe, and you are a true pessimist. So rather than dissect your quotes, I instead have mildly dissected you, my reason being the nature of this course. It is psychology and finding out what makes us all tick… and I have to say I agree with your call on these two people. Well done," he said, trying to take the sting out a little.

The bell rang, and the class quietly filed out, each in their own philosophical thoughts.

Six students in the same psychology course, all from different backgrounds, different journeys, different personalities, different baggage, and different stories to tell.

Let's flashback to Penelope at eight years old, at home in Ellsworth, Michigan.

Mom and Dad Perfect (now there is an impossibility if ever there was one: parents can never be perfect. In fact, nobody can be perfect. But that's another story!) were sitting at the dinner table with their six children, in Ellsworth, not too far from Ann Arbor, where the University of Michigan was. Elaine was a housewife, no time to be anything else with this brood, although she used to have ambitions to being a comedian, when she was young and beautiful, though she still looked good, and *she* thought she was hilarious! And Dad, well, he was a mechanic, a good one, but not a top one, and not rich by any means, but not poor, and he made sure his children never did without. Penelope's mother was a sensible type of person, black and white as far as moral issues went, but always fair. Her dad, Tom, was a bit of a dreamer, always wondering about the ship that passed in the night, what he could have done with his life, a real 'if only' type of personality; but he was satisfied with his lot, his wife and his children. Together they were chalk and cheese, but somehow it worked.

The dinner menu always followed the days of the week, and today was Tuesday, so it was liver and onions, spinach and corn on the cob. The table was noisy, as you would expect, everyone talking at once, shouting for the salt, the ketchup, pass the napkins, get me a drink of milk, hey get me a Verners (a native Detroit drink) with ice… hey you, move over, you're nearly on top of me, can I have more corn please, and pass the butter dish, babble. A cacophony of utensils, loud opinions, and chewing, not necessarily in that order. It was chaos. But warm and comforting.

Penelope loved dinner time. She could sit quietly, as was expected of her, being only eight and not really allowed to be taken seriously in the serious subjects that were often thrown back and forth around the table during the half hour of communal living. What no one realised was that she was perfecting her art of 'people reading. 'She would study every face, in repose and while they were speaking. Interesting. Nobody knew how much they gave away both in body language and in their faces, she thought, nobody knew how transparent they were, except me… and this is how Penelope defined herself, even at this young age. "I am a people reader," she said proudly to herself, and held on to it because after all, everyone, especially in a large family, needs their own voice. She had her own voice, but back then it was silent.

"Hey, Nicholas," said their dad, Tom, in between mouthfuls of liver, "how are you doing at your new school, are you fitting in okay?"

Nicholas was Penelope's older brother by seven years and he had just turned fifteen. He was a moody young man, and always seemed to begrudge his father, looking down on his choice of trade.

It wasn't anything he said out loud, more of an attitude that Penelope easily picked up on.

Tom had no idea, as he was lost in his own little dream world most of the time. He drifted in and out of his kids 'lives, throwing out questions like this over dinner, and thought it was enough to constitute communication and caring about their welfare, however surface it was. He didn't get it. He thought Nicholas and himself had a good relationship. And they did, except for that important word - r.e.s.p.e.c.t! - this did not exist from Nicholas to Tom. And at today's dinner, this seemingly innocent question sparked Nicholas off, making him fly off the handle and blurt out quite angrily, which did seem to come out of nowhere, the following tirade.

"Yes, father. I am doing fine because I have something burning in my gut. Something valuable, something worthwhile, something I will never ever lose. It's called AMBITION. You never had it. You just decided at some point you were going to work on cars. Wow, big dreams, eh? And then proceeded to have child after child, never even attempting to maybe start your own business, maybe go up a step on the scale of income, maybe, oh God, I don't know, maybe you could have at least tried to be SOMEBODY. I do love you dad, but by God, I will do more with MY life, and that is a promise!"

And then, silence.

Tom did not retaliate. He ignored this outburst, putting it down to teenage angst, and continued to eat his food quietly, looking at something only he could see, hanging in the air.

This was a key moment in young eight-year-old Penelope's development as a people reader. In that instant she saw how her father pushed reality away with both hands, chose to not hear, chose to stay asleep, and chose to simply get by. Wow. Interesting. And Nicholas. He is a snob, and not just money wise. Intellectually wise as well. I wonder what his life will bring him, disappointment? Who knows? Will he end up as 'nothing, 'as he thinks the man who sired him is? Or will his dad's life end up inspiring him and pushing him to his personal limit? Who is the loser here, who is the winner? Only time will tell.

She would dwell on these questions for the rest of her life, always searching for the answer, but always, yes always, since the age dot, in fact probably before she was born, she was a 'glass half full 'person; but with a difference. One who did indeed see both sides of the equation.

Flashback to Max Morose, age ten. Apartment in Brooklyn.

Max was toying with his greasy fried eggs over easy in the cramped tiny kitchen with the tiny breakfast table, which the three of them, Max, his mother and his grandmother, just about had room to gather around at mealtimes.

His mother, Natasha, pretty and still slim, but had seen better days, was looking over at him with such love that it was a physical force, often overbearing for the young boy, even though he was only ten. He was aware of how claustrophobic it all was and yearned to be free of this emotional trap, although he couldn't articulate this yet. It was just a feeling at the edges of his psyche. He did however adore his mother with every fibre of his being and therein lay the dichotomy of the development of this most unusual child. A most perceptive child to be sure.

The kettle was boiling, as the soft click clack of knives and forks filled the room.

"So Max, what do you plan on doing today? It's the weekend, no school, you should go and see some of your friends, play outside, go to the park, play baseball, ride your bike, but do something! Don't just sit around and let your life pass you by. This is not a dress rehearsal. Today is the first day of the rest of your life and believe me, I know what I am talking about. Look what happened to me. Just look what happened to me!" She cried out, breaking into tears, while taking a crinkled letter out of an envelope and reading aloud… reading aloud, for the third year running.

"Dear Natasha,

I am sorry to inform you that our marriage is over. I have not been happy for a very long time and have met somebody else. As soon as our divorce is final, we will marry.

I wish you and Max a happy life together.

To be honest, with your overbearing mother around, WE never stood a chance.

Kind regards and I hope you will be happy.

I tried.

Yours sincerely,

William."

Max looked at his grandmother, who always managed to look stern, rarely smiling. She rolled her eyes to the ceiling, shrugged her large shoulders, and pointed to the date on the newspaper lying on the table.

Oh my God, he thought. The anniversary of my parents' divorce. Every year I forget about it and every year it happens again. She gets all upset AGAIN, gets out that letter, again. And cries, again. How many tears can she shed for this man? My dad. My dear old dad. For sure, he isn't coming back. I for one am glad. He was very quick with his fists, oh yes, he sure was, and I got so very tired of explaining the marks on my arms and shoulders to my teacher during gym class. Good riddance, I say. What a shame though, Mom. What a damn shame that you let this cold hearted, admittedly good-looking man ruin your life. I feel so sorry for you. I guess that's why you love me so much. How sad, and what a waste of an existence. You poor woman.

These grownup thoughts were internal, never to be spoken, but etched deep inside Max's heart and mind. What he said aloud was "Oh, come on mother, come on... don't cry, please don't cry. You know how much I love you. I hate to see you so upset. Why don't you put on the nice blue dress of yours, you know the one, the one that brings out the colour of your eyes, put a little red stuff on your cheeks and lips, and go downstairs to Betty's for a nice chat. You always feel better after that. Just please don't cry anymore... he isn't worth it, Mom, he's just not worth it. And we are better off without him. You don't need him in your life. I am your 'man 'and I will take care of you for the rest of your life, that I can promise you," he finished solemnly.

Natasha looked gratefully at the son she adored, so like his father, glanced at her mother sympathetically, because in all honesty, the failure of her marriage had nothing to do with her.

26

More to do with the weakness of the cad she had hitched up with. She blew her nose, dried her eyes, gave her son a big kiss on the cheek, and quietly left the table to do exactly as Max had suggested. A nice chin wag. Just what was needed.

Max could not help but be cynical in this situation, and as sorry as he felt for his mother, the bigger part of him felt anger at her weakness. How can you love somebody who walked all over you? How can you keep that feeling alive? How can you keep hoping, dreaming, caring, imagining him returning to the scene of the crime, to take you in his arms and tell you that he was wrong. Oh yes, he thought, I know the scenario in my mother's mind. And it goes like this. He rides in, handsome and smiling on a white horse. He dismounts, bows down and begins, "Oh my dear Natasha. I should not have gone away. You are the one for me. And my wonderful son Max. I'm so sorry for beating you, it was only the anger at myself that I was taking out on you. A small part of me was just a little jealous of this new male human being in my life. I really want to make it right again." Good God, it was exhausting trying to be positive about it all… and Max put the mental brakes on and screeched to a halt in his mind. It was much, much easier to just be realistic. Or negative. Whatever. The man was no good, no use in pretending anything else. I shall never forgive him for what he did to my mother. Never! Nor will I ever, or should I ever, forgive him for what he did to me. Bastard!

Max's glass would remain half empty for the rest of his life.

Max would unknowingly continue to look for a father figure for the rest of his life.

Max would not trust love for the rest of his life.

Max would remain a pessimist for the rest of his life… or would he?

Present day, back at college.

As they filed out of the classroom, they gravitated towards each other, slowing down, waiting for a chance to actually speak, introduce themselves and shake hands.

Lillie sidled up to Peter, tapped him on the shoulder and took the initiative.

"Hi, Peter, I am Lillie. Nice to meet you. Where do you originate from? I would guess, by hearing you speak, it's Boston, am I correct?"

"Why yes, Ms. Lillie, and I always move forth with great vim and vigour," he replied, quoting one of his favourite speeches, which he'd seen on old newsreels replayed every year on the anniversary of the assassination. The late, great President John F. Kennedy had the most unmistakable Boston accent, which he mimicked quite easily.

"I am from New York, born and raised in Greenwich Village. Both my parents were true beatniks; you know, poetry, bongos, coffee houses, so it's no wonder I turned out alternative. Shall we get a coffee?"

And off they went, heads together, chatting away ten to the dozen.

Edmund, who was naturally very shy outside of his family environment, was looking down at the ground, not paying attention, and banged straight into Patricia, whose books went flying.

"Oh my oh my oh my. I am so sorry. It's Patricia, isn't it? Let me help you pick everything up. God. I am so clumsy, like a bull in a china shop, my dad has always complained about that, ever since I was a little boy," he babbled, while picking everything up and putting the books into Patricia's arms one by one until finally he was done and standing, and they were eye to eye… Boy. She was tall, as tall as he was. Funnily enough though, Edmund was not intimidated; he found it quite attractive in a way… challenging for sure, but sexy with it, in fact, sexy and vulnerable. Now that's a great combination.

Looking straight into her beautiful blue eyes, he was stunned into silence. He knew his cheeks were crimson but there was nothing he could do about that. He always felt uncomfortable around attractive women, yet he had no idea why.

"How do you do, Patricia. I am Edmund Woodhouse the third, and it is my pleasure to make your acquaintance," he said, sounding very formal indeed.

"Hello, Edmund. I am Patricia Hodges, the first… but don't let that bother you. It doesn't bother me. I am happy to be one of a kind, and being this tall kind of guarantees it, if you know what I mean. So, how do you like the class, how do you like the professor, how did you end up here at this college, taking this course?"

Patricia was the enquiring kind of person and wanted to know everything about everybody, but she gave nothing away about herself. Not that she didn't trust people, more that she didn't trust herself. She had always been a very vulnerable person, too sensitive for her own good, which was why she took the pessimistic cop out. It was her emotional armour to get through this painful world. Painful for her, anyway.

Edmund, not used to a woman taking the lead, was on the back foot for sure, and waiting for what she would suggest next, never dreaming that he could make the first move. Or that he should make the first move.

"I found your choices and explanations quite interesting. Although the opposite end of the scale from mine. How about we go for a drink and have a little conversation about it… what do you say?"

And off they went on the road of discovery as to who the other one was. Anything could happen.

Finally Max and Penelope were left alone, standing just outside the college's main entrance doors. It was electric, it was awkward, it was unavoidable.

Penelope took the initiative. "Hi there, and may I call you Max? It's nice to meet you. Loved your quotation choices, very clever. I think I am going to like this course very much. The professor is interesting, don't you think? There is certainly more to him than meets the eye and he is very, very perceptive. It's all in the eyes. Don't you just love observing people? Especially when they don't know you are watching them. I am a bit of a people reader… been doing it since a child… and, and… and…"

Max was staring, really staring. Directly into her eyes, which made her shut her mouth immediately.

"And hi to you, Penelope. Same back atcha. I noticed you the very first day, mainly because you were sitting at the end of the row, the same as me, and 'watching'… which is also one of my favourite things to do. And, can I say, I do find you very interesting. Even though we are opposite as far as negative/positive

29

goes. I believe we have a lot in common. Whadaya say" - he was lapsing into Brando again - "shall we have a drink or two?"

Both parties were intrigued and both parties were willing to begin their journey. Off they went to the local pub where most of the students hung out, and there they found a quiet corner, both ordering a large G and T with ice, of course.

And they began to talk and talk and talk...

Flashback to Penelope aged fourteen, in Ellsworth, Michigan.

Penelope was lying on the floor playing with her nephews, who were six and eight years old. The eldest sister by ten years, Louise had produced these beautiful specimens, after having a wedding in a big church with no expense spared, her high school sweetheart by her side. Romping all over the floor in the living room was one of life's pleasures. Innocently adorable. She could just eat them both up.

Louise entered the room with her shopping bags, and sat heavily on the couch, looking troubled and distant.

"What's up, sis?"

"Oh Pen...I just don't know. I wake up every day under a cloud. I can't figure it out. I am married, I have two wonderful kids, we have a nice home, plenty to eat, we have friends to go out with, so really I have nothing to complain about, except I AM NOT HAPPY..." There, she had said it out loud.

Penelope and Louise always had this connection. Even with the age difference, they just 'got 'each other. Often the younger felt like the elder, especially in this moment. This was serious, so Pen dug deep and tried to help the best she could.

"Okay. Let's start with the basics... do you love your husband?"

"Yes. But I see now it's more like a brotherly love. Kind of late to realise that one, eh!"

"Are you sorry you have kids so young? Has it tied you down?"

"God knows I love them both, but Pen, I don't know who I am. I never did. I just rushed into this whole thing because I thought it would make me independent. But it did the opposite. It strangled me. Damn."

"Let's cut to the chase. Are you having or are you thinking of having an affair?"

Louise's face turned crimson.

"Yes, I am thinking of it, and yes, I have... I have discovered sex for the first time. Can you believe it... two kids later and I now discover sex! If it wasn't so tragic, it would be funny."

"Is it love, Louise, or just sex? Now be honest."

"Well... I am not in love. I am in lust. Can't seem to get enough. We meet once a week, when you babysit and I do my 'shopping.' Mmm... mama's got a brand new bag, eh! Here I am making jokes and I feel awful. Awful because this affair has highlighted my discontent. I will say it again. I AM NOT HAPPY. What am I going to do?" Her tears began to fall.

It was another important moment in developing Penelope's interest in psychology, and the tie between mind and heart, and how far apart they can be. Reading her sister was easy and she couldn't help but do just that, observing the many emotions riding across her sister's face. She got married too young, she had no life yet, no experience, not even sexually, so had no idea what she liked in that area, tied down now with two kids. Feeling trapped by her own decisions; and on top of it all, married in the Catholic church, from which there was no return. She let her cry on her shoulder a little longer, and then tried to give her a helpful answer.

"Okay. This is what I think. You know I am always here for you. I love you very much. You are a special, beautiful person, inside and out. And don't ever forget that.

"An affair is not what causes a divorce. It is just the symptom. If you are not happy now, you are not going to find it anytime soon. This kind of feeling does not turn around. You have fallen out of 'in love'... in fact, it's quite possible you were never 'in love 'at all. You must think long and hard about this. This will affect your life for the rest of your days. Stay, and you will have to compromise and accept that you will never have that 'in love ' feeling. Only you know if you can live that way or not. Leave, and you will have your freedom, but along with that freedom comes the guilt. And honey, there isn't anything like good old Catholic guilt to accompany you down the road of the sinner. I suggest you end this affair now. You have some serious decisions to make."

"Pen, you are such a wise old soul. You know me so well. I love you too."

This scenario would affect Penelope for the rest of her life. She loved her sister's husband, having known him since she was a child, and she knew that he adored his wife and that this would kill him. At the age of fourteen, she decided she would never be a divorced woman. In fact, maybe she would never marry at all. This scared and scarred her emotionally and from this moment on, she had a block on her heart.

Flashback to Max Morose aged sixteen.

Many years had gone by since his father walked out the door, never to return.

Max tried to convince himself, daily in fact, that this was a blessing in disguise. But somehow, it never quite reached his heart, and buried in there was a deep loss of a father figure.

There were a couple of teachers at high school, one who Max gravitated towards. He was tough but kind, clever but also vulnerable, and he seemed to genuinely care about Max's education. His name was Mr. Standon. He taught history. He was good-looking and blond with beautiful blue eyes, and more than a little charismatic.

Mr. Standon and Max often met up by 'accident 'in the cafeteria after the school day had finished, and they often sat together, drinking coffee and having long discussions about anything and everything.

After about a year of this, Max felt comfortable enough to confide in Mr. Standon the situation with his father, and his deserting the family. Once he started to talk, he couldn't stop, and in fact he became, surprisingly, very emotional. Mr. Standon listened quietly and respectfully.

At some point, the atmosphere changed and became electric. There was a subtle shift of concern from Mr. Standon into something else. Almost sexual. Max wondered if he was imagining it and started to feel very uncomfortable in himself. He fell silent.

As he sat there, he realised Mr. Standon was in fact gay. He also realised he had been unwittingly sending out the wrong messages. Oh no, what now?

Mr. Standon grabbed Max by the shoulders, catching him off guard, and tried to pull him closer.

Max pushed him away, standing up quickly, but stopped himself from laying him out, which was his natural inclination. Instead, he took a beat, and looked down at the handsome man sitting uncomfortably looking up at him. Waiting... waiting. For some kind of signal that it was okay. It wasn't okay. Max was not a homosexual. Finally regaining his calm, Max spoke quietly and deliberately so there would be no misunderstanding in the future.

"Mr. Standon... I am not that way inclined. If I gave you the wrong impression with our conversations, then I am sorry for that. I guess I must have done, or you would not have made your move. I can see that you are very embarrassed and very disappointed. I hope you can put this down to an incomplete forward pass, and that we can remain friends. I do enjoy your company. And again, I am sorry if I misled you in any way."

There was nothing more to say at this juncture. They parted company, each with their own thoughts.

Max had just made an important discovery. If ever there was a perfect moment to try the other side, that was it. He liked the man, found him attractive, looked up to him, enjoyed talking, all the boxes were ticked. He did not find him sexually attractive. In fact, he had never found a man sexually attractive and most likely never would, and if he did, well, he would deal with it. And that was that. At this point I am one zillion percent heterosexual, he thought. Job done. Onwards and upwards. Oh boy... that was crazy!

Back in the pub, the clock was ticking away, and Max and Penelope showed no signs of leaving. The G and Ts were rolling along nicely, as was the conversation. They truly did hit it off, and this was a first for both, being guarded in the heart area albeit in different ways.

"So, Max, tell me a little bit about yourself... not the standard answers you gave in class. I would like to know you a little better than that. I find you very interesting," and before she could stop her mouth from saying it she added, "and very cute!"

Shit, why did I say that, she thought. How embarrassing. She blushed. Actually she blushed very easily. Most people found this one of her most endearing qualities.

"Well, Pen... can I call you that? Not too familiar is it?"

"Not a problem. I, Pen, full of ink and ready to always make my point... And I'll call you Max, shall I?"

"I do like your sense of humour. What exactly do you want to know? Let's see... well, I am an only child, parents divorced since I was very young, a mother who never got over it, raised with her and my grandma in a small apartment in Brooklyn. I was glad when my dad left because he wasn't very nice to me..." Max gathered speed, getting louder, quite unexpectedly, seeming to forget where he was and who he was with. "Yep, used his fists sometimes... yep. Glad to see the back of him, for sure, absolutely. Best thing that ever happened to me. If he was still around now, with me all grown up, I would beat the shit out of him for what he did to me as a child. Yep, glad he is gone."

Max shut up.

Long silence, slow sipping of the drinks, more silence. Max was feeling a little exposed and Penelope even more curious.

She looked compassionately at Max and said, very softly, "Methinks ye protesteth too much."

Silence, sipping, clinking of ice cubes.

"Okay, Miss Penelope Perfect," Max said a little harshly, trying to regain some control after his rather revealing outburst. "Your turn... quid pro quo, and no bullshit either. So sister, shpillda beans or da kid gets it." He was lapsing into another old favourite of his, Humphrey Bogart. He was a sucker for the old movie stars and the old dialogue. He thought there was a certain charm in the dialogue of that day.

"Right, okay, here we go. Me, hmm, well, I have two sisters and three brothers, mom and dad of course. From a very early age I realised I needed to find MY voice, not just as one of the clan. MY voice. I needed to be alone, mentally and physically, and found a way to do just that. Even though there were people in every corner of the house, I found my secret place where I could sit in silence and think, even moving my bedroom to the basement when I was in my teens. Mentally, I simply retreated into my psyche, alone with my thoughts and observations. From about the age of eight, I began to 'read 'people. I would watch their expressions as they talked, which were often in direct contrast to what they were giving lip service to. I would analyse their postures, their opinions, their triggers. I guess you could say, finding *my* voice was all to do with analysing *their* voices, if that makes any sense. One thing that has been the engine that drives me, I always knew I was different. Don't ask me how I am different. I just am. So! Here I am, Penelope far from perfect… yet Perfect. Ta da," and standing up, she did a little jig and a bow.

And just like that, the ice was broken and it would now be phase two. What that was going to be neither knew; a road untravelled, no map, no compass, just blind faith, and curiosity, to lead the way forward.

"Well, I don't know about you, Pen, but I am tired. Shall we call it a night?"

They swallowed the remains of their drinks, took a long look at each other, then parted company and went back to their respective dormitories.

Class 3

Monday morning arrived without a sound. The psychology class quietly filed into the classroom. Penelope noticed that Professor Handover was sitting at his desk, not bothering to rise, looking a little troubled, a little unsteady, and maybe just a teeny bit drunk. Very strange indeed. He seemed like such a proper, upstanding gentleman. This was very out of character. Maybe she was reading it wrong, but she didn't think so.

Well, this should be an interesting lesson!

Slurring ever so slightly, the professor began.

"Let the class begin. Welcome to you all. Now, putting aside your quotes and your assignments for the day, I would like to try a little experiment. We are all formed by what we witness, good and bad, in our childhood, and indeed, the way we process what we witness, good and bad. And the very fact that you are all interested in this course means you have some demons in your past that you need to work out. This is not a bad thing at all. In fact, quite the opposite. You are all intelligent and have enough of an enquiring mind to want to go the distance. So, today, off the cuff of course, we will each of us tell a story of an incident in our childhood that has never left us. I purposely did not want to give you any time to prepare for this but of course whoever goes first will be the guinea pig so to speak. To be fair, I will start."

Hmm, thought Penelope. He is bothered, and definitely a little the worse for wear, but holding it together, just. Well, my ears are wide open.

Professor Handover stayed seated, which was unusual for him, and began to talk, softly, which was also unusual for him.

"I want to tell you a little story. It's about a small boy and his mother, who by the way, were very close, as many mothers and sons are. It is how nature intends it to be. Fathers and their little princess daughters, mothers and their little prince sons.

"Now, the father/husband was a classic physical abuser. The abuse was always instigated by alcohol. A little background on this damaged individual; sorry, don't mean to lead the jury, but there is no other way to see him. Or maybe there is. This will all be up for discussion shortly.

"He - let's call him George, just to give him a name - was a ravaged-looking young man, but you could still see traces of handsomeness around the edges of his demons. And this was his downfall. He thought his looks were his passport to a good life, not bothering to get a proper education, falling in and out of love, in and out of bed, taking easy labour jobs just to earn just enough so he could date girls and consume alcohol. It was a never-ending cycle of good times and hangovers, until he met his future wife, who we shall name Monica. He actually fell in real love; they married and had a son. It was after the child was born that George started to see the uselessness of his way of life, but instead of trying to change it, he just became bitter. Bitter that Monica had somebody to love, and jealous as hell that his son was such a sweet, good-looking toddler. Basically, he felt completely invisible. And again, without trying to lead the jury, the real problem was he was invisible to himself. And so, when the boy, who I will just call 'the boy', was about five years old, the physical and emotional abuse began in earnest. This scenario was the boy's blueprint for life.

"Now, the mother, Monica, was a very sweet natured woman, who would not hurt a fly. She came from an upstanding, old fashioned, good Catholic family which instilled in her that marriage was for life, and that two horses pulled the cart together, come what may. She loved George very much and, as most women do, thought she would be the one to change him. She saw potential, she saw a good man buried inside; the operative word being 'inside'. The good man she saw had no chance of getting out. Every drinking binge pushed him further down the black hole.

"The birth of her son, the boy, enabled the marriage to continue, as having a child does, it gives you hope. But the cycle was established, and it would not change... abuse, forgiveness, tears, blame, shame, guilt. And every other emotion in between.

"Here is how it normally went. George, after work, doing whatever job fell into his path, would return from the bar, take off his coat and shoes, stomp into the bedroom, wake up his wife, demanding food, drink, sex, whatever, and if she dared to not oblige quickly enough or answer back, the beating would start, and keep going until the drink took over and he would pass out on the bed.

"The boy would stay in bed, knowing instinctively that he should. And that if he showed his face, his father would get even madder. He knew from experience it would not last long, maybe fifteen minutes tops.

"One night though, his father must have overdosed on self-loathing, anger and alcohol, because the beating continued for at least half an hour with no signs of him stopping. The boy got worried. So he quietly went into the room for the first time and stood, as manly as he could, at the end of the bed, wearing his five years with dignity.

"His dad stopped hitting his mother, miraculously!

"There was an uncomfortable silence, both mother and son wondering what the hell would be next. Dad/husband looking thoughtful, which was very unsettling.

"Then, dad/husband smiled a menacing smile, and everything made sense again. He said, very softly, almost singing it, 'Okay, here's what's going to happen. We're going to play a little game.'

" 'You, boy, I am going to hit your mother again, and you are going to stand there and watch. If you cry, I will hit her again, if she cries, I will hit her again. If neither of you cry, I will stop. Do you understand the rules?' The question was rhetorical.

"Now, let's stop right there. Let's examine this scenario. Let's apply logic, and psychology, not necessarily in that order, and of course a little compassion, but that should not get in the way of your judgement.

"Question number 1.... Who is this man, what do you make of him? Raise your hand if you wish to answer."

Edmund's hand flew up of its own accord, as did Peter's and Max's.

"Okay Edmund, you first, what's your take on this?"

"Well sir, I always try to be non-judgemental until I have all the facts. We have no idea what his back story is. Not that it gives him an excuse, of course. I would ask some questions about this man. What kind of a father did George have? What kind of a mother? Was there abuse in his childhood, because as you said at the beginning, we are all affected by what happens to us both physically and emotionally as we are growing up, and this stays with us a lifetime. I need more details."

"Okay, Peter, your turn."

"Okay, besides being horrified at any parent doing something so cruel to a child, making him watch and not letting him cry, so psychological damaging - poor thing - I too would like to know the back story. Nobody is born bad. There must be something in his background to explain this kind of behaviour. I say nobody is born bad, but maybe some people are... but I would say normally, something happens to turn them the wrong way, so in a way I agree with Edmund's answer."

"And you Max, how do you feel?" That should do the trick, he thought to himself, saying how do you 'feel 'to Mr. Don't-show-anyone-anything which he wore on his sleeve in place of his heart.

"Right, this is how I feel about it. I don't care if he had a psychotic father who beat him every day, and a mother who was on the game and brought her work home with her sometimes, I don't care if he grew up with no warmth or compassion and very little knowledge of what's right and wrong... I don't care about any of this because there is no excuse for abusing a child, none whatsoever. Whoever he was, I hope he got his comeuppance. Evil, abusive and just plain nasty."

Max sat down heavily, looking very angry. Obviously Professor Handover's story had struck a nerve.

"Okay, thank you Edmund, Peter and Max. Let's get some female opinions about this man."

Penelope, Lillie and Patricia tentatively raised their hands.

"Patricia, you go first please."

"My immediate reaction to your story was deep sadness, not for the beating as such, but, as Peter just said, for the psychological damage it must have done. Forgetting about George for a minute, my brain travelled further down the road. I would love to know how the boy turned out. How he righted things in his head. What career did he choose? Did he succeed in life, did he marry, did he have any children, did he have male friends, did he trust women? I would absolutely love to have a one-to-one conversation with the boy."

"And you, Lillie."

"Mixed emotions I'm afraid. What he did was horrible, beyond comprehension. I want to dig deeper too. I would love to have a conversation with George. I have a million questions I would ask. And for that matter, the mother too. I need to know reasons for this behaviour. The whys and wherefores. I want answers so I can try and understand the path he took. A nasty man for sure, but mind wise, kind of interesting, in a Ted Bundy kind of way. He was methodically cruel, but obviously also intelligent, even with his choice of the psychological games he played. Cruelly fascinating."

"And you, Miss Perfect."

"Besides the initial sadness at such a sad tale of abuse... I believe absolutely that this George learned his behaviour as a child, and since this was his 'normal', he could not shake if off when he became an adult, and therefore, as happens in most cases like these, he repeated the pattern. He should have had medical help, and I hope he got some. He had serious issues. The mother, bless her, should have walked away, with her child. And the boy. Oh boy. I can only imagine what scars this left in his heart. I wonder how he survived it, if he survived it. Did he ever share his story with anyone or did he bottle it up inside? Was he able to function in this world? Did he find a job that suited him? Did he go into a career that dealt with these issues?"

Clever girl, thought Professor Handover, looking long and hard at Penelope. Their eyes met and he knew that she had worked out that this was his story, and that he was the boy. And, because he had indeed had a couple of gin and tonics at lunchtime, he felt himself wanted to unload the entire thing, in the name of psychological discovery of course. And, he thought, if I go the distance with this, exposing myself, that will signal to these six gifted students, which he had decided they were, to dig deep and expose themselves too... and then... and then... this will be a hell of a learning curve, maybe even a healing for one and all. God knows, he thought to himself, I would love to get rid of 'the boy ' once and for all.

In all honesty, the professor was drawn to studying, and eventually teaching this course, because of his childhood pain. And that pain was as intense today, when he was fifty, as it was when he was that boy. Maybe it was finally time to speak about it publicly. Maybe this was the right group of people to speak about it to. Maybe he was finally able and ready to speak. God knows he'd waited long enough. It was a serious decision to make. He paused. Decision made.

"Okay. Here we go. In answer to your questions." He leaned dramatically on his desk. "Well, first Max, you hit the nail on the head. George did have an abusive father who beat him regularly, and indeed a mother who was on the game, who did sometimes bring her work home. This was his blueprint. His father luckily died quite young at the age of fifty, with causes related to alcoholism, and his mother was beaten to death, aged forty, by one of her customers. George ended up being sent to a foster home for about five years, where unfortunately the abuse continued, sexually and emotionally. He left legally at sixteen, having found work in a local shop, where a room over the store was thrown in as part of his wages. He was free, physically, but not emotionally. Never would he be free emotionally.

"So, there you have it, a portrait of a confused and angry young man who could either stand tall and make something of himself against all odds, or seek revenge. He chose the latter.

"With no qualifications, this handsome, angry young man worked, drank and fucked - excuse my French - not necessarily in that order. He didn't really care deeply about anyone or anything. He just wanted to live his life the way he wanted to live it, no ambition, just happy to amble along at his own pace. And then he met Monica.

"Monica, as I said earlier, came from a strict Catholic family. She was a good-looking woman, well built, every bit as attractive as George was. She lived around the corner from the shop that he worked in and fancied him from day one. She constantly thought up excuses to go and purchase things. George

41

tried to ignore her; she was a little too young and inexperienced for him. He liked older women who knew what he wanted and needed. Eventually she worked her innocent magic, and he found himself in love.

"They married, rented a small apartment, and began their lives together. Monica fell pregnant within three months, and nine months later the boy was born. This was when George's anger surfaced. He had a married a truly nice, supportive woman, who always tried to see the best in people. She was now the mother of his son, and an excellent one. She kept the apartment spotless, always made sure he had clean clothes, and a nice meal when he returned from whatever meaningless job he did, never questioning him, always loving him. The problem was, George felt like he was living a lie. He knew his background; he knew there were holes inside that could never be filled. He felt like he didn't deserve this good woman's love. Why should he - even his own mother hadn't cared! So he set about trying to destroy that love because he did not know how to receive it.

"Every night George found himself struggling to contain his fury and rage. And every night he came closer and closer to losing it, until he did. Returning from the pub, much the worse for wear, he noisily stumbled into the living room/ kitchen. Looking around at the cheap furnishings, the dishes drying in the sink, the clothes rack with freshly washed laundry drying by the Aga, the toys on the floor, the crib taking up too much room, oh God the futility of it all. Who am I? What is the purpose of all this? Then the drink took over.

"He marched into the bedroom, grabbed his wife by the hair and pulled her out of bed, and started to hit her. He was beating her for every wrong that was done to him in his life, and God it felt good. Monica knew it was best to just shut up until he either stopped or passed out. She was smart enough to realise he had totally lost control, and anything she said would just add fuel to the fire. Fifteen minutes later, he was done and sound asleep on their double bed which was really a glorified single bed. Monica went into the bathroom to look at the damage, shellshocked and numb. What the hell just happened, she thought? Repaired herself as best she could, and went to check on the boy, who pretended to be sleeping, lying back down in bed, finally falling into a fitful sleep, certain that George would not remember a thing the next morning... She was right. He remembered nothing. His hangover was legendary, and slumping over his coffee he looked at Monica and asked her, 'What happened, did you fall over or something?'

"The boy had heard it all.

"This was the beginning of their nightmare.

"So, boys and girls, I would like to stop my story right there, to be continued of course, after all, there must be a conclusion, yes? What I would like to do now, using this story as a reference point, search inside yourself and find *your* emotional trigger point. I am throwing this at you because, if it is a true life-altering experience, you shouldn't need to think about it. It should be right there on the edge of your mind. Now, who would like to go first? Come on, don't be shy."

Edmund raised his hand.

"Well, sir, I can tell you mine immediately. So here we go...

"I grew up in a wealthy home, full of art, expensive furniture, and servants to do your bidding. We ate, just us three, mother, father and me, at a dining table that could seat twelve. I always wondered why they had such a big table, it wasn't like they entertained, well, hardly ever anyway. It was a cold atmosphere, not feely touchy, more intellectual. Even from a very young age, basically as soon as I could communicate, we discussed, we debated, but there was always a distance.

"As a child, although I could not articulate it, I felt it. You could say I grew up in a loveless atmosphere. I never felt easy in their company. And I began to depend on my communication skills to get me through this family and through this world. One night I heard loud voices emanating from my parents 'bedroom, which was very unusual. They were never that emotional about anything, they never exposed anything. So out of character... so of course I was curious, and I carefully tiptoed within hearing distance and shamelessly eavesdropped. I was only seven years old. I heard my mother crying - my mother, crying?! - then I heard my father's voice say very loudly, 'How dare you blame me for anything? How dare you. You passed Edmund off as my own son all these years. I

43

never had any idea. If the truth hadn't come out in the blood tests, would you ever have told me? I don't think so. EDMUND IS NOT MY SON!'

"At that point I ran away back to my own bedroom, hid under the covers and cried my eyes out.

"I have never felt like I belong anywhere since that evening."

Silence ensued, until Professor Handover cleared his throat, quite pointedly.

"Thank you, Edmund. I am sure we can all sympathise with the hurt this must have caused you, and so young too. In my opinion you have done very well in being able to understand yourself within this situation, and indeed being able to expose yourself like you just have. May I add, to consider yourself an optimist in the mix… very well done.

"Can I ask, is this incident what drew you to my psychology course?"

Edmund sat back down and softly replied, "Yes, that is the reason. I have been looking for 'me 'ever since that day, and I hope this will help me find out or at least come to terms with who I am. I never pursued this subject at home. I felt it was best not to know the cold hard facts, but maybe in hindsight this was a mistake."

"Right… who is next? Patricia. You look very deep in thought; will you share your 'moment 'with the class?"

Lofty Patricia sat up very straight. With her sensible haircut, her sensible ensemble and sensible shoes, she looked stern and vulnerable at the same time, yet dignified. She began to speak in a slow, apologetic manner, which was who she truly was. Slow and apologetic. A classic, heart-on-her-sleeve personality.

"Well, Professor, I don't know if I have just one moment, rather a series of repetitive incidents happening to me, and I am talking about heartbreak here. I guess it began with my first love. I was fourteen and fell hard in it. He was seventeen and should have known better. He was my first love, and one year later, my first lover; underage or not, I was more than ready." She paused at the memory.

"We shared everything, we really connected, and I allowed myself to be taken over in a way. I would do anything for him, told him I loved him all the time, hung on every word he said, waited for his phone calls, put his name all over my schoolbooks, 'I love Chris 'was everywhere. I was a hopeless case, a true romantic with no thought whatsoever about any danger in how I was feeling. For two years he was my guy, I honestly thought we would marry. Then at sixteen, he found somebody else, and just like that, I was history. But here is the hard part: when we broke up, he explained to me that I was too needy, too clingy, saying I love you, I love you, I love you, like a broken record. And that I wasn't quite clever enough, or pretty enough for him. Well, as you can imagine…" Her cheeks turned red now, with humiliation at the memory. "I was emotionally destroyed. He stripped me of my confidence and made me feel second best. And to be very honest, because that's what this discussion is about, I have repeated this pattern ever since. Maybe it's a case of knowing and expecting this to happen with every guy I date, and then making sure it does happen. I need to learn the lesson; I do know this. But it's hard. Hard and painful… I know this and accept it, and therefore it's comforting in a crazy kind of 'been here, done that, know how it feels 'kind of way. Is it any wonder I consider myself a pessimist? I don't think so. The end."

"Interesting, Patricia, very interesting. Later in this course we are going to be delving into the breaking of patterns. It's something everyone needs to learn how to do: it's human nature to repeat, but patterns can be broken. Thank you very much for your honesty. And by the way, you *are* pretty enough, and you *are* clever enough."

Encouraged by Patricia's honesty, Lillie thrust her hand in the air before she could change her mind. It's sink or swim, she thought to herself, God can I really talk about this?

Lillie was exotic, with her European way of dressing, unlike anyone else in the class, as she was well aware: today's ensemble was skintight black jeans paired with black leather boots, a striped black and white t-shirt, and a jaunty black beret on her head.

She stood proudly and took the floor.

"Well, Professor, I am a little reluctant to speak, but internally I know I must try to because, at the very least, it's a

45

beginning to my quest to understand ME a little better. And I am not being ambiguous, I am being honest. So rather than pick out one incident, although, as I am speaking, I am sure one will come to the forefront and make itself known… my learning process has been a series of family and friends trying to put me down for simply being different, trying to make me fit into their version of me. Which I never could do and can't do now! It has been a lifelong situation for me and for want of a better word, jealousy springs to mind. I have been surrounded by people trying to dim my light from day one. I AM clever, I AM artistic, I AM talented." She paused, then added, loudly and angrily: "I AM DIFFERENT, SO EXCUSE ME! And I don't see why I should be punished for it when surrounded by lesser individuals suffering under their own delusions of grandeur, who have nothing better to do than to try and drag me down with insults and negativity and take out their frustrations on me. I can only surmise that it's because I do not conform, I do not react, I just sit quietly with a blank look on my face, and this infuriates them even more. Notice I say 'they' - the great 'they'. Who are 'they 'and why in God's name should I even care? They don't!"

There was a pause as she struggled with herself, and then decided to go for it, arranging her attractive face into a semi-smile. The best she could do at that moment. These were uncharted waters for her.

"Okay. There was this one time… I was at a party, let's see, must have been around fifteen years old… I was with someone I thought was a friend, a girl named Lulu. She was one of those extremely popular people and seemed to attract people of both sexes easily. Everyone wanted to be close to her. But I *was* close to her. We somehow got separated, mingling with different groups of people. As I finally managed to extract myself from a rather boring mixture and made my way over to Lulu's circle where she was holding court, I happened to overhear her say 'Oh God yes. That is so true, Miss Holier-than-thou. Thinks she is so smart, looks down her nose at everyone with that blank look on her face. Hahaha. And she thinks we're friends! The truth is, I feel sorry for her. I don't think anyone really likes her.'" There was a long pause, and Lillie's sad face, remembering the confusion, changed to defiance, and then blankness, in that order.

"Yes. There you go, that was my life changing moment. I retreated into my uniqueness, my talent, my creativity, and decided from that point on it would be me, myself and I. And voila. A pessimist is created." She paused. "Lulu and I were finished after that evening. I wonder who she's trashing now? And, just to draw a line under things, from that moment on I accepted that I just did not fit in anywhere. A square peg in a round hole, or vice versa, depending on your way of thinking."

She stood there lost in her thoughts for a few seconds, and then Lillie sat down.

The professor coughed. "Lillie, I had you pegged as a 'hard to read 'person from day one, and I believe my impression is correct. I knew you had a different story to tell. Yours is most interesting and if you are up for it, we can all dissect it piece by piece and help you discover that hurt young woman who shelved her feelings, turning them into arrogance, and disappeared into herself where she thought she would be safe. This is your first step towards rebirth and many steps will follow in these discussions. Thank you very much for that. Very interesting. And I for one can't wait to dive in myself, metaphorically speaking. I'm a good swimmer!

"Well, students, can I just say that we have made an excellent start. I applaud you for taking this emotional chance and baring all with people you hardly know, like having a session with a psychiatrist. Sometimes it is easier to talk to a stranger than to somebody you are close to. And so, we continue. Peter, you're up next."

Peter stayed in his seat, looking from side to side, as if he did not know what to say. He was dressed in blue jeans, coupled with a white t-shirt, white belt, and white shoes. Quite sporty looking. Handsome and fit if you like the clean-cut look. He rose slowly and began in a quiet monotone voice, quite unlike his usual jocular tone. There would be no jokes today.

"Okay… so, I honestly can't think of any one moment as such and can only describe my upbringing. There were three of us, elder sister, elder brother and me. It was what I would describe as a 'surface 'family. Nothing was argued, nothing was questioned, all was calm and peaceful, and well… just nothing. No ups, no downs, just existence. I don't mean no love, we all knew we were loved, and I don't mean cold either, just blank. There was a certain distant closeness between us, if that makes sense. It seemed like nobody cared to dig beneath and find out what made us all tick.

"I remember one dinner when I decided to push the boundaries of conversation. I was always a curious person, anyway, always asking questions. So, I blurted out between mouthfuls of mashed potatoes, 'Mom, who were you before you met Dad? Did you have dreams, what did you want to be when you were a little girl? Are you satisfied with your life?' Yes, I know. Pretty serious stuff from out of left field eh?

"I'll always remember the silence that descended around the table. Forks in mid-air, surprised looks, embarrassment which morphed into closed faces, and then… nothing. Five minutes went by. We all kept eating. Finally, my father piped up and said, 'Peter, this is not an appropriate dinner conversation.' And that was that. I didn't try again, not even in private with my siblings. I just accepted that this was how my family was wired and got on with it. I did find my own way of coping was being able to crack a one liner and make everyone laugh. This at the very least gave me some kind of voice and raised the level of boredom, however briefly. I guess that dinner was my moment, although I didn't realise it until just now. And, truthfully, the reason I am in this class is because I really do want to dig inside myself. I have so much curiosity about the workings of my mind, the feelings in my heart, the sadness, the joy, everything. I need to know what makes me tick… tick tock tick tock tick tock, whoops, ding. My time is up! And there you have it. Peter, coping with life as he knows it!"

He sat.

'Thank you, Peter. Your story, and what lies behind it, could be described as passive aggressive, which is a wonderful tool to help you through traumas with no one being the wiser. My immediate response to you would be: were you then, and are you now, aware you are doing this?

"Can I be so bold as to add, I think beneath that comic exterior there is a volcano of anger ready to erupt, and I think that's

48

why you are here. The emotional lava inside of you is ready to spurt out the top. And that is exactly what taking this course will enable you to do. Very glad you shared that with us, very glad indeed. Now relax, your dissection is not due for a little while yet. Time enough for that… tick tock tick tock." He chuckled. It was becoming a catch phrase for the students and their teacher.

"And now for our final two guinea pigs, Max and Penelope. Now, don't take offence, either of you, we are all, including myself, guinea pigs here. We are on the road to self-discovery. It may be awkward as hell, it may be embarrassing, humiliating, tearful, whatever the adjective… On we go. Max, enlighten us with your story. We will save Miss Perfect for last."

Max stayed seated, which was very telling. No swagger on show. He was a little uncomfortable. Closing his eyes, he sat back and tipped the chair as far it would let him before falling, sighed a few times, swayed his head side to side, and slowly began to speak.

"As you all must be aware due to the few titbits I have dropped during these classes, I did not have a wonderful upbringing; in short, an abusive father who left when I was young, an overbearing mother, who I love dearly, and a hard as nails grandmother, born in a different generation. So, raised by two females with no man to put his macho foot down, at least not after he was gone anyway. But he had put it down and planted it in my ass more times than I can remember, before he left, so you could say his footprints left their mark. And to be honest, I had more of his footprints than I've have had hot dinners. Now the challenge, for the sake of this discussion, is to find that one moment that altered the course of my life, but I don't know if I can do that. Truly. I just cannot pick one out. I would say it is a combination of my father treating me like an idiot and his personal punching bag, my mother doing just the opposite, like I was the saviour come back to earth, and the sun shone out of my ass, and me knowing I was neither. These two opposing views left me with an emotional void inside, a place that can never be filled. I am empty of love, empty of feeling, empty of peace. I am however full of intelligence, curiosity, and ambition, all of which I cover with a suit of arrogance. I got a scholarship for this course and that is why I am

49

here. It seemed like a good opportunity to journey into a personal and dangerous black hole - and that black hole is me."

Silence all around, waiting for Max to break it. He smiled wryly and softly said, "Classmates, I am an emotional virgin, so be gentle with me. As you all know, you never forget your first time. That's the end of the Max Morose story for today. Tune in next week, same channel, same time."

Professor Handover stood up at his desk and slowly walked around to the front, then came to stand directly in front of Max, gazing at him with directness and compassion, knowing how difficult his monologue had been.

"You, Max, are a very interesting character. First, despite your naturally rebellious attitude, you were able to share with us on a very honest, and probably a little embarrassing, level. These kinds of things are never easy to talk about. Even though none of this is your fault, it feels like it is. I understand you on a gut level, more than you may realise. And you are right, this is your opportunity to exorcise your demons. And Mr. Morose, you have a head start, because you recognise you do have demons. Many people don't, in fact I would say at least eighty per cent of the population are in denial.

"You are here, you are ready. I applaud your bravery. It is so much easier to stay asleep. And now for our final exposé of the day. Penelope, you have the floor."

Penelope stood up to her full height of five foot two, gathered her personal space around her so it fitted nice and tight, took her dramatic pause and slowly swept the room with her analytical eyes, finally coming to rest on a spot just above the professor's head. She began.

"I am from a large family, two sisters and three brothers, which comes with its own set of challenges. The good part is that you have no need to go outside for companionship with so many siblings to choose from. The bad part is, who are you? You need to find your own very special voice within the family unit. I found mine quite young. I found I had a talent to people read and have been doing it from about the age of seven, and I must say, I am good at it."

To make her point, she looked at each student in turn, with the look she had perfected over many years… straight into the soul. And each recipient looked a little nervous, including the professor.

"I am going last, which is both a blessing and a curse. A blessing because I have had time to assimilate and a curse because I have had time to assimilate, maybe rejecting or revising my first, real, instinctual moment.

"My eldest sister by ten years married her childhood sweetheart and quickly produced two children, who I adored and often baby sat while growing up. I was very fond of her husband, Davey, having known him since as long as I could remember.

"Louise and I had this strange relationship: you could say we were the closest siblings in the entire family, which is unusual because of the ten year age difference. But that's what it was. Long story short, she finally concluded that she only loved Davey like a brother, and was never 'in love' with him, and wanted to divorce. I remember when it was finally said out loud and accepted by all of us as a fact of life. We were all sad, Louise included, but she did not want to live the rest of her life not being in love. Which I could totally understand. The sad part is, for Davey, she was the one true love of his life. He could not change this feeling, and neither would time. I guess my moment came when he wandered into my bedroom one evening, a few days after the bombshell had dropped, sat on my bed, and collapsed, literally collapsed. He was a broken man, lost with no viable return, a one-way ticket to heartache, and two children in the mix. I comforted him as best as I could, but this scene scarred me forever. When he finally left my room, hopefully a little lighter, though I doubt it, I sat on my bed for a long time, thinking things through. Decisions were made, emotional decisions, if that makes sense, because, as we know, emotions are not controllable. But what I learned, and I am sure you will agree, Professor, you can control your reaction to your emotions, if that makes sense!

"Anyway, I decided I never ever wanted anyone to love me so much that me removing that love would kill them. I did not want that kind of power over anyone. I could not stand to see someone, anyone, so broken. It touched me deep inside. Too deep, in the place where we should never venture unprotected. I realised that I was too sensitive. Now. What to do about it. I certainly could not exist wearing my heart on my sleeve, a target for every misery that may come into my sphere. Oh no… I had to do something!

"So I put a mental shield around my heart from that day forward. Not a block you understand, just a protective layer. Yes, I have been in like/lust/love, yes, I have been liked, lusted after and loved, but NEVER have I let myself go to the point of no return or allowed anyone to go to that point with me. Not sure I was successful on that score though. So far, for me, it's worked. In a way, I am rather like Max, a virgin, although not technically speaking," she added, blushing crimson and looking extremely cute.

Penelope stole a quick glance at Max, who was staring directly at her, which naturally, the professor caught; in fact, caught easily.

"And that, I would say, was my moment, a moment I have been living ever since. And before you ask, Professor, it is one of the reasons I took this course, but not the only one. I do have a natural curiosity about the human mind, and the conflicting emotions of the heart, and I do love discovering what makes people tick… so Peter. Tick tock tick tock back to you, in fact to all my fellow pupils. Let the healing begin."

Penelope smiled at him to take any misconceived sting out of her comment, and sat down, with a proud aura around her.

"Thank you, Miss Perfect; and that was perfect, in every way. It leads to a very important conclusion to today's class. This is for everyone to digest.

"It is fine to find a way to not be hurt, hiding, ducking, diving, camouflaging, masquerading through the world in the way that you think protects you best. But just take this on board: if you can't get out, nobody can get in, and if nobody gets in, YOU will never get out!

"Your assignment this week is to delve into your own personal moments that you have shared with us all today and see if you can find a way to move past them, find a way to make them work for you and not against you. Find a way to break your pattern. Throw out that comfortable pair of jeans that don't fit anymore. Find a way to take a brave new step into the world you previously knew as yours… and I will tell you the conclusion of the story I told, which began this class today.

"It's been a heavy, insightful hour, let's see where we go next. I'll bring the map; you bring your own compasses. Class dismissed."

Everyone filed out quietly, each in their own personal space, afraid to look around or communicate, knowing that they had all exposed themselves. They all felt emotionally naked.

Flashback: Penelope, fifteen years old, in the second year of junior high school.

Penelope had been seeing Steve for three months now. She liked him. He was nice looking, tall, slim, brown hair and brown eyes, smart, compassionate and good company. They had a lot in common intellectually. They hadn't slept together yet, but were damn close to it. Tonight was decision time, and she knew it. She had arranged to pretend to spend the night at her best friend's house, Steve's parents were away, and protection was purchased. The evening awaited. Could she go through with it, or would she chicken out at the final moment?

They were lying on the couch in front of the television in the main lounge of Steve's family home, as they had done many times. Kissing, kissing, and more kissing, touching, exploring, going to first and then second base. But this time with a difference. Third base was being tested out for the first time with the overhanging promise of a home run. Steve took Penelope's hand and led her upstairs to his bedroom. The moment had come.

Without taking their eyes off each other, they both undressed silently and lay on the bed together. Penelope noticed the pack of three on the bedside table. Oh my God. Here we go.

This was the moment. Penelope was a virgin, and it did not happen easily or without pain; in fact there was a lot of pain. It was not pleasant at all… but finally, after some difficult thrusting, he was in. One, two, three, and it was over. And then he started to cry.

"Oh my God, that was so beautiful. I love you; I love you; I love you. I never want to be without you. Promise me you will marry me, Penelope. As soon as we turn eighteen. You are the love of my life."

And just like that, it was over. In Penelope's mind it was like watching Davey, her elder sister Louise's husband, sitting on her bed and sobbing his heart out. It's funny how incidents like this, from a long time ago, leave a residue in your heart and soul. This was just too much pressure. She did not want to be responsible for this man's happiness.

Of course, she said nothing aloud. Just quietly got dressed, and asked to be taken home as it was lot to take in. Steve obliged, of course. He was one of life's gentleman.

This began the pattern of like, lust, love, and run for Penelope. Something she could never quite shake off.

Present day.

Edmund, Lillie, Patricia, Peter, Max and Penelope all retired to their separate dormitory rooms after the class. It had indeed been exposing and exhausting. They all needed private time to assimilate and digest.

Edmund sat at the small desk in his room looking through an old diary that he had started at the age of eight, and still regularly added to. He found himself wondering about his family blood lines. The name Woodhouse: that was not who he was. His mother's maiden name was Fraser. His dad's parents, his grandparents, her grandparents 'great-grandparents. Hers was a long line going way back in time that she loved to tell him about, although it was not as prestigious as that of his 'father', who was not his father. So, he thought, where does that leave me?

He resembled his mother, everybody always said so, and as he looked at faded photographs in the album he had taken with him to college, he saw they both resembled his maternal grandmother, which gave him some comfort, and a sense of belonging, at least looks wise.

The issue that today's class had brought up for him was whether he should, this late in the day, ask his mother for some facts about his real dad. He had always buried it at the back of his emotional cupboard, but maybe now was the time to take it out and bring it into the open. The questions on Edmund's mind were: Do I or do I not want to find out who my biological father is? What good would it be? Would I be better off not knowing? Is he still alive? Would he want to see me?

Yes indeed, today's class had opened up the proverbial can of worms.

It was with these thoughts that he finally fell into a troubled sleep.

Patricia sat quietly on her bed. It was around 8:00 p.m., and she, like Edmund, had a photo album with her. It was the only thing she had taken with her when she left her family home. In it were all her prized memories, including a school photo of Chris, the boy who stole her heart, and her pride. It still hurt like hell to think of him, which is why she rarely did. But today brought it all back. She stared for a long while at the photo and brought him back to life in her heart and mind. Her mind drifted with thoughts.

I wonder if he got married; shit, maybe it was to that girl, the one he threw me over for. I wonder if he has kids. I wonder if he is happy. I wonder if he ever thinks about me. I wonder if I will ever fall in love again, like I did with him? All-consuming. In fact, I wonder if I will ever fall in love again. Because, in all honesty, I don't fall in love, I fall 'into 'love - I lose myself every single time. What was that old saying from the Prophet, oh yes' ...Remember to let the winds of heaven dance between you.' Good God, that is so true... why do I collapse into each relationship? Is it a lack of self-confidence that began with Chris, or was it in me anyway? Maybe it is just the way I am wired; maybe I am a hopeless romantic; or maybe I only pick out guys who will repeat this behaviour because it is what I am used to, and validation is a wonderful thing, isn't it?

Well, I am in this psychology class and hopefully I will get some answers eventually.

Goodnight Chris, wherever you are. You bastard. You ruined my life. But I am determined to turn it around, and I WILL!

And with these thoughts, Patricia feel into a deep sleep and dreamed of a knight in white armour coming to rescue her on a white horse, flowers of kindness, and an ocean of respect. He was perfect.

Lillie, oh Lillie, oh Lillie, wherefore art thou Lillie? She hit her room with a vengeance, kicking the door open, throwing her coat on the floor, and kicking the table over, which spilled this morning's cold cup of coffee all over her freshly washed bed linen. She sank down on the couch, switched on the radio, crossed her feet and sulked. First, she did not like exposing herself, although at the time it seemed very natural. She had always been a closed shop. Always. In fact, just the opposite of Patricia, who went in search of a repeat of her first love at every opportunity. Lillie never wanted what happened at that party to happen to her again. And if she kept her heart closed, her thoughts to herself, and her anti-people badge on her sleeve, she should be safe. Right?

No. Not right. Who am I kidding, she shouted to herself. I am so damn tired of being an island, so damn tired of closing myself off from the world, so damn tired of being scared to feel anything. So damn tired.

What I said in class was completely true. It just flew out of my mouth before I could help it. I could feel the compassion swirling around, and to be honest, if felt nice. Maybe - and I am saying MAYBE - it's time to let myself out and allow people to come in. Okay. Let's leave that there for tonight.

She poured herself a small glass of white wine and fell asleep on the couch.

Peter was relaxing on his bed, reading an autobiography, his preferred choice of reading. He liked these kinds of books because they combined truth with the history of the times they were written in, politics, religion, attitudes, upbringing, everything, a perfect combination. He was reading with a book light clamped onto the hardback cover. He loved to read. In fact, he didn't read books, he ate books. But tonight, he was reading without really reading. His mind was elsewhere, and he kept having to go back and rc-read what he thought he had already read. He turned off the light, closed the book, plumped up his pillow, and just sat there. His emotions were all churned up for some reason; not his normal way at all - he was just not the churning type. Many questions were creeping around the edge of his mind. Why did nobody in his family care about sharing?

Then, a eureka moment! Oh, I like that. I think I will write a poem to share at next week's class. In fact, I think I will write it right now, he thought to himself, and he got up from the bed, grabbed a notepad and began. No time like the present. Let's nail this sucker before it buries itself again. He began to write.

Max went to the local student bar. He needed a G and T or two. He did not like exposing himself at the best of times. Not at all. But today flew in like a hurricane and he found himself swirling around in winds of discontent, and that discontent was with himself and how his past was always ready to drag him down into a swamp of anger, and feelings, things he didn't need or want. He was so sick of this. He hid it most of the time, rarely talked about it. But Max, being a deep thinker and a 'no bullshit 'kind of guy, knew that somewhere inside his soul, he needed this, needed it badly. Otherwise, he would not have shared a single word. He said things today in class that he hadn't told anyone before, and that was a shock to himself.

So, what am I going to do about it? I've got a week to either go forward or find a way to retreat. The choice is mine, he thought to himself while finishing his second drink.

Then he put the thoughts away, and walked back to his dormitory with that rebellious swagger that was all him, hoping he would - or could - come to the right conclusions.

Lying in bed, thoughts were running around his brain. Don't retreat this time, Max, don't run away, don't be scared, you can do this, damn it. You CAN do this.

It was with these confusing thoughts that Max finally fell asleep.

Penelope didn't know what to do with her evening. Should she go for a walk, go for a drink, a quick bite to eat, read, listen to some music, or sit and think? Sitting and thinking won. She sat on the edge of the bed. Just as she had sat on the edge of life for as long as she could remember. Always waiting for a bomb to explode. Always ready to run into the safety of her secret heart if things got too close. Why? A simple question: why?

She sat there, straight up and silent for over an hour, not moving a muscle, as she mentally listed the reasons she was like she was.

And then she stopped thinking, and like a robot, got undressed, into her favourite extra-large t-shirt that doubled as pyjamas, turned down the bed, put her pillow just so, climbed into bed and turned off the bedside light. She closed her mind, then her eyes, then fell asleep.

Professor Handover laid in his canopied single bed, which he had rescued from the local antique shop, in his functional apartment provided by the college, three small rooms including the bedroom with bathroom, a small sitting area, lounge, and a kitchenette, which was more than ample for his bachelor needs. He had personalised it with a few items including a photo of himself as a young boy in his mother's arms, sucking on a pacifier, with an angry looking father, tall, imposing, looking on with a cold glare. He had considered cutting his dad out of the photo but then, taking his psychological expertise to heart, realised that would be ridiculous, because you cannot cut the memories out. This snapshot, the only one he had kept, remained intact in a plain wooden frame. "Always something there to remind me," he sarcastically chuckled to himself.

He took off his shoes, his jacket and his tie, draping them over the wooden chair in the corner, walked across the small black and white throw rug, and into the 'sitting 'room;" Humph, they should have called this a standing-room-only room," he chuckled to himself again. Profess Handover was a closet comic, but only he was aware of it!

Resting on the shelf of the small book cabinet was a bottle of Famous Grouse, half empty from last night and this morning's journey into his demons, and tonight he would journey again. No class tomorrow, so he may as well drink himself into emotional oblivion and worry about the hangover tomorrow.

He sat there quietly on the brown leather couch that had seen better days, thinking, Oh boy, this couch is just like me. I've seen better days too. Sipping, thinking, remembering, talking out loud to himself…

I wonder what has triggered all this. Why now? I went into this job because I really thought I had dealt with all these issues years ago, and could help other people find their way in this emotional maze which we call life, by teaching psychology.

And since he was alone, as usual, there was no one who could add their two cents, which led to the next thought…

That's it, isn't it? This group I am teaching has triggered something in me, has shown me a snapshot of what I have become. A lonely man, no wife, no family, no friends... and horror of horrors, having a nip before taking the class. Never have I done that before! Something about these six people. Somehow, they have managed to get inside me and open the door to my heart. And why? I barely know them... well come on, Professor, you're the expert, he said out loud to his inner self, how ironic... come on!

He sipped his drink slowly, then grabbed his pen and pad of paper, which were always nearby so he could make notes for the next class. Feeling very philosophical, he began to write, in big bold letters.

REALITY CHECK FOOTNOTE TO MYSELF:
THERE ARE NO ACCIDENTS IN LIFE, YOU GO THROUGH WHAT YOU'RE SUPPOSED TO GO THROUGH, YOU MEET WHO YOU ARE SUPPOSED TO MEET, AND WHAT HAPPENS IS SUPPOSED TO HAPPEN.THERE IS A PLAN, THERE IS A MAP YOU MUST FOLLOW, EVEN THE MISTAKES... THEY TOO ARE MEANT TO HAPPEN. LIVE YOUR LIFE, FACE IT HEAD ON, DON'T LET YOUR LIFE LIVE YOU.

Professor Handover was challenged in both mind and heart. It seemed to him that he was given these six students for a reason: it was supposed to happen, he was supposed to be the teacher, and he was supposed to be questioning his own life. His mind was ready and waiting, his heart was uncomfortably curious. Onwards and upwards.

With these thoughts he had a few more snifters, finally rolling his head back on the couch and falling into a deep, untroubled sleep.

The week passed slowly for the six students. They were happy to be in their own company, and did not seek each other out. There was much to digest, and much to prepare for next week's class, which came around much too quickly for most of them, including the professor.

Class 4

Edmund, Lillie, Patricia, Peter, Max and Penelope filed quietly in and took what were now their normal seats. It was a sombre looking class, very quiet, very thoughtful, very, shall we say, ready... but ready for what?

A cough came from the doorway as the professor entered and went to the front of the class with a few determined strides.

"Good afternoon, class. Now I do know that you will all have spent a quiet week, thinking and digesting what we talked about last week. And, can I just add, so have I. It has occurred to me that we are going on a very special journey together. To have gone this deep so quickly. Well, that can only be a good thing, in my opinion; scary, unsettling, but good."

Looking slowly from face to face, he settled on Peter.

"Peter, would you like to share with us your thoughts on last week's revelations and what you think about them now, having had time to digest properly what was said."

Peter stood up, and opened his notebook, looking uncomfortably confident, if that's possible. Flicking a stray piece of hair back from his forehead, he began.

"Okay... instead of explaining my thought process, I decided to write a poem, with the intention of sharing it today. Because it says it all, much more eloquently in a rhyme, don't you think? Anyway... here I go.

CARING AND SHARING
by Peter Pendergast

Sitting at the table
Breaking bread
Staring at the ceiling
Lost in the void
Of words left unsaid.

No one seems to notice
No one would dare
To break this silence
This cold war, his to bear
No one seems to care.

Glancing face to face
The boy digests
The absence of feeling
Hollow beating in his chest
No one seems to care.

Caring and sharing
Till death do us part
This vow of silence
This pain in my heart
Wish my life could start.

The end.

"Phew." Peter sighed softly and sat down.

"Phew indeed," said the professor. "I am so impressed. First because you cared enough about your self to write a poem about your feelings, second because you were brave enough to share it with us, and third because it is a beautiful poem... and do you realise what you have accomplished? You have taken the first step out of your emotional prison, the prison that was imposed on you by your upbringing. Well done. Very well done.

"I hope the rest of you are prepared to be just as honest. Peter, cliché though it may be, today is the first day of the rest of your life.

"Right. Who is next? This not an express train but an exposé train." He chuckled. God, I am funny, he thought. "All aboard!"

Edmund spoke up." Me, sir. I am ready to share my thoughts with the class.

"When I got back to my room, I went to my memorabilia, diary, photos, stuff I always take with me when I travel. I was looking for clues as to who I am. My mother's maiden name, for example, looking for some kind of connection, some kind of clue, anything rather than not knowing anything. I was relieved to see a big family resemblance from her side, gave me a good feeling. The question that bothered me was, why did I not pursue answers? Why did I never ask the questions? Why did I just let it go after overhearing the fact that my dad is not my dad? Why? I have had the week to ponder this. I think I am just plain afraid. What if I do find out who my real father is, what if he is a jerk, a low life, with no brains or humanity? Or maybe he was just a one-night stand, and my mother knows nothing about him, and never had any communication, and maybe he doesn't even know I exist. Or what if he is a very intelligent man, who did well for himself, has a family etc? Do I go down this 'what if 'route and try to find answers, and if I do, what difference will it make to the person I am today? This was the decision I pondered for the last six days.

"And I have made my decision.

"I am an adult; I am who I am. Whoever fathered me makes no difference whatsoever to the person I have become and would not make a difference now. I think I will keep my illusions of who he may have been, be proud of the man I am, put it all behind me and keep on walking. I am a good person.... I like me... and in fact, I was able to shake hands with that little boy who eavesdropped on that private conversation. And, if you go along the 'everything happens for a reason 'train of thought, I was supposed to hear it, I was supposed to feel how I felt, how I feel now, and finally I was supposed to let it go, now, in this classroom. So goodbye childhood demons, hello happy adult. Ta da."

Edmund sat, looking as if a weight had been taken off his shoulders. And it had!

"Well, Mr. Edmund P Woodhouse the third, welcome to the world. Psychologically I am giving you a gold star today. Well thought out. You didn't take any shortcuts, you examined all your options, and you got to the finish line emotionally intact. It will be interesting to see how this monumental realisation and decision affects you from here on in. I think you are in for a few surprises. You are now ready not only to receive but to give as well. Thank you. Hard to believe we are only four classes in, and we have come this far. Brilliant. Just brilliant."

Penelope put her hand up.

"Yes, Ms Perfect?"

"Professor… can you please finish *your* story. I am sure we are all dying to hear it.

"Please!"

"Well," he answered, "I suppose it's only fair; after all, I am on this exposé train too, and even though I am the teacher, I have a gut feeling that there is much for me to learn from all of you, and I am honest enough to admit it. Okay. You asked. So, here we go.

"The boy was me. Well done, Penelope, I know you already guessed this. I loved my mother unconditionally, as she did me, but I could not forgive her for her weakness at allowing this to happen to her, to us, for not leaving when she had the chance. I always wanted to be someplace else, away from the ugliness. I only wanted to be with my mother, safe in her arms. From as far back as I can remember I never felt 'safe'. This boy grew up and grew away emotionally from himself and found a niche in which he could fit emotionally, if that makes sense. This boy delved into psychology and found answers to his psyche in a language he could understand. This boy forgives his parents, both, understanding that they brought their own baggage to the table.

"This boy has chosen to teach, to help, to lead the way to emotional equilibrium, no matter what you have been through, and this boy has been to hell and back!

"Also, most importantly…" He paused. "This boy has 'chosen 'to be alone in this life."

There was an uncomfortable embarrassed silence in the room, which lasted a good five minutes.

The professor coughed.

"And to put a line under my story, even though this boy found answers to his questions, they are only truly answers in his mind; his heart remains a mystery, and he is still unable to cry.

"And before anyone points it out, yes, I do find it more comfortable telling my story in the third person - one step removed, you see, which is the only way this boy managed to survive at all."

Wiping his glasses and looking suspiciously teary, he said, softly:

"Who's next?"

Penelope raised her hand.

"Yes, you have a question?"

"Professor Handover, if I may be so bold as to ask… WHY? Why have you chosen to be alone? Do you have no hope or desire for a relationship of any kind? Aren't you lonely?"

"Good question, Penelope. Hope and desire are elements of existence, some things we attain and others we don't. Oscar Wilde said, 'There are two great tragedies in life; one is not getting what you want, and the other is getting it.' That's where I stand.

"I prefer to leave the door to my heart closed. Survival, you see. Having been raised in a world of lonely, I don't know any other way to live. And to thrust this upon an unsuspecting partner would be selfish and unforgivable. So yes. I have chosen to be alone, yes, I am lonely but content with my choices… ninety-nine per cent of the time. And one per cent of unhappiness is not bad considering the options!

"Right. How about you, Lillie? Are you ready to purge your inner soul?"

Lillie stood up, reluctantly, not at all sure what she wanted or was going to say. She made up her mind this would be unplanned, and she would shoot from the hip… and if nobody liked it, tough shit!

"Okay, I have been doing a lot of thinking, a lot of remembering, a lot of allowing myself the luxury of allowing hurt to re-enter my heart, which I have not done for a very long time. The question I kept asking myself this week was why did I care

64

what 'they 'said, what 'they 'thought? Are we vulnerable at any age? Does this caring disappear as we become comfortable in our skin? Which leads me to the big question. Am I comfortable in MY skin? Have I ever been? This arrogance I have affected: I am different, I don't need you, I have my own brand of talent, I am me. Stay away and keep your insults for yourself you bunch of losers! Is it all a big act, some kind of joke? And, if it is all a big act… WHO THE HELL AM I?"

She sat down with a huge thump.

Professor Handover stood directly in front of Lillie and looked deeply into her eyes. She really was an interesting, attractive woman, full of depths even she herself was not aware of. He was feeling something unusual, an emotion he could not quite put his finger on. Could it be he was developing feelings for this woman? Oh my good God. Wouldn't that be ironic? Quickly burying this emotion, a trait he had down pat, he said," Lillie, I sympathise with you. For the sake of the course, and me being your teacher, can I say, psychology is all about cause and effect. Which is the cause, and which is the effect? That's the question here. You are right to now be questioning exactly who you are as your disclosures have shaken your foundations, but I must say, it seems they were built on quicksand! You must get to the source. Were you always different, truly one step out of time with everyone else, or did your experiences while you were growing up force you into this shut-off corner you call home? I think this is why you are a little angry. You don't have the answer, and that is the answer. I make you a hundred per cent correct. WHO THE HELL ARE YOU? And my dear, the only one who can answer that is you. But we will all certainly be happy to help you to get to your destination, with a few pleasant stops along the way. Think about that this week in your down time. Which came first, the chicken or the egg… sorry to 'lay 'that on you." He chuckled at his own joke. "And Lillie, just before I move on, can I say that you and I have a lot in common. It seems we have chosen the exact same route for getting out alive. Ah… but what did we leave behind?"

He clicked his heels together with a smug, self-satisfied smile and bowed to his student, as if he knew a secret, and perhaps he did. Watch this space, he said to himself.

And, for a fraction of a heartbeat, Lillie saw a real smile grace his lips. But it disappeared as quickly as it had arrived. Still, she saw it! Watch this space, she said to herself.

"Who would like to go next?"

"ME!" Penelope blurted out, much to her own surprise. Lillie's dramatic tale had stirred her emotions up. Emotions she didn't know were there.

"Okay… total honesty time.

"I went to my room after class, like we all did, and I could not settle on what to do, which is always what happens to me when just sitting still and thinking is required. I knew I had some canyons to explore, a navel to contemplate. I sat a long time remembering my ex-brother-in-law and the pain I witnessed first-hand, and how it affected me, deeply. I remembered my first boyfriend, my first time, not easily forgotten, how dependent he was on me, how clingy, just too much in love, hard to live up to, I have many flaws, I am not perfect. Hahaha… I AM PERFECT. Sorry. It was just sitting there. Had to go for it… but I digress. There is nothing humorous about any of these stories we are sharing.

"I remembered boyfriends who followed, friends, families, and found myself wondering: who am I close to? Has anyone ever had the inside track? Have I ever let anyone get that close? And the answer is a resounding NO. Saying that though, I am not lonely, have never been lonely, quite a social butterfly. I obtain boyfriends and friends very easily. Problem is, I am prepared to let them go, just as easily. So, one thought leading to another, I considered the option that maybe I am cold hearted, which made me very uneasy. Then I listed different reasons why I never allowed myself to go the distance with anyone. Mentally, repeatedly during the last six days. And they are good reasons, valid reasons, logical reasons… but all the reasoning in the world cannot stop you from getting to your true destination. And after all, this was the assignment this week. Think about your defining moment and go from there. So I will conclude with the self-discovery I made… and as much as I am a people reader, and pride myself on my ability, I never properly read myself before. I am doing so now…

"I AM AFRAID.

"There, I said it. Now maybe it won't be such a scary thought anymore. After all, it's not a sin to be afraid."

Penelope sat down looking like a six-year-old little girl who's just been told off. A very appealing look. All five students and the professor sympathised. There was a collective sigh. All that was needed now was a circle and a prayer!

"Thank you very much. I applaud your thinking process. This was not easy for you to do as your particular escape has always been to find out what makes everyone else tick, tock…" He glanced at Peter. "And another reference to your tick tock tick tock, Peter." He chuckled, repeating the phrase which had become a mental time bomb for everyone. "While you, my dear Penelope, are busy, reading everyone else, you have neglected YOU. And eventually this will come back and bite you on the ass!

"Are you all aware that I am using the word 'escape 'within these exposés? And the reason is, it is human nature, when faced with insurmountable problems, to find a place to hide… so first we escape, and then we hide, until something, someone, some situation, forces us out of our comfort zone. And, my dear, if you are willing, next week I would like you to give me ten good reasons, written out by the way, why you are afraid.

"Right, two more left. Patricia and Max, who wants to go first?"

They both looked at each other. Neither one seemed anxious to go. There was a pregnant pause, and then Patricia took the initiative and stood up.

"Can I just say, Professor, it occurs to me that everyone's story is related to either loving somebody else or loving ourselves. We are all stuck in the L word, love. What is it about this 'condition 'that it is so daunting, so scary, yet so complete, so final. I am starting with this analogy because my problems are to do with being in love and then being jilted, never easy at any time, but particularly difficult as a teenager when you are insecure anyway. Goes with the turf. My time this week was spent reliving Chris and I, when we were a couple. I got out old schoolbooks - haven't done that in years - and conjured up the entire thing, replaying it in my mind, feeling it all over again. Yes, I was humiliated, I was wounded in my self-esteem. So, my question to myself, in the past six days, was why do I keep repeating this pattern? I don't want to be hurt, I don't want to be rejected, yet give me a line-up of ten men and I will pick out the worst prospect for loyalty every time. I have knack for it. I know it's not as shocking or traumatic as the other students here, quite a basic problem really; but to be honest, which I always am, I am just a girl, waiting for my hero to come and rescue me. Outdated though that may seem, I am who I am. I wonder if I do repeat this pattern because I am used to this kind of pain, I even expect it, and maybe I am afraid of letting go of this because then what will I do with my heart? Maybe I will have to use it and not abuse it, properly for the first time, heaven forbid! Which leads me to the obvious conclusion that I am totally aware of what I am doing, walking into each heartbreak of my own free will, and expecting yet damning the predictable outcome. And, since I am an open person by nature, which is why I hurt so easily, I welcome all options for my future emotional well-being.

"But let it be said, I don't want to change who I am. I don't want to hide my heart, I don't want to act cold, I don't want to develop a façade. I happen to think that my softness and vulnerability are the most precious attributes of my character; I just want it to stop hurting me so much!

"Wow, I said a mouthful, didn't I?

"There you go, everyone. This is why I am here. I mean not the only reason obviously. But what drew me here. My moment was simply loving and then being rejected and left wondering what's wrong with me. I guess I need to develop some kind of 'ego' - but I've got to say, it doesn't come naturally. Maybe pride is a better word for what I am looking for. My heart is on my sleeve, and I would like to put it back where it belongs. Maybe I should change my name to Rapunzel, then I might have a chance.... hahaha."

She sat softly down with a smile that didn't quite reach her eyes. She looked quite beautiful in that moment, quite naked, so to speak, which surprisingly and unexpectedly touched Max's heart.

"Thank you, Patricia. This is a psychology course obviously, but there are no limits on what is important and what isn't; the point is to delve into ourselves, and find those key moments, recreate them, remember them, feel them, and analyse them. We have all been drawn here for different reasons, yet the same reason. We are all searching for the parts of our personal puzzle, so we can make all the pieces fit. You need not think your story is any less valuable than anyone else's here. It's all a matter of perspective. In fact, yours, Patricia, is perhaps pure, unassuming, compelling and a basic problem of life and human existence, plain and simple. It's a four-letter word called love… you fall easily, always for the wrong one, hurt easily, cry easily, then carry on, not so easily, into the next disaster. And love is perhaps the most interesting, frustrating and satisfying psychology dilemma in the entire universe. Who of us can explain it properly, who of us can understand it, who of us has control of this, who of us hasn't been rejected? I myself find it hard to even understand what creates attraction in the first place. Is it one psychosis recognising a similar one, is it opposites attract, or is it simply a chemical reaction? In fact, your story affected me at a very deep level. I would like to try an experiment for next week's class. Can you all do me a small essay? 'What Is Love? 'I will also contribute my thoughts on the subject; now there's a Freudian slip. My 'thoughts', when I should have said my 'feelings'! I think I will start there with my musings.

"Thank you again Patricia… or should I say Rapunzel.

"Okay Mr. Max Morose, you're on."

Max slowly and coolly stood up, façade in full view, shrugged shoulders, t-shirt hanging over his blue jeans, attitude at the forefront. Taking his moment, sneer in place, armour shining, he looked around the room slowly, stared at the professor a moment too long, and then, he sat back down.

No one spoke. An uncomfortable confusion tainted the atmosphere.

He then arose again, without the façade, without the ego, without the swagger, in fact, looking quite 'normal'. Dare this word be used?

"Sorry for my little visual display there. What I have to say has all to do with me wanting, and more importantly needing, to let go of my alter ego, the person who makes it possible for me to bulldoze through life, to never get close to anyone because me, myself and I do not need to get close to anyone. I am self-sufficient, I am my own best friend, I don't need anybody.

"I am a rock. I am an island." Not only a fan classic old movies, he was a fan of classic old hits too. "Thank you to Simon and Garfunkel for writing my theme song. Hahaha. Or maybe not.

"Within all this swagger that I possess, and don't I know it, I discovered during the last week, digging deep down where I do not like to go, a highly emotionally soul, who needs to find a way out of himself, out of the disappointments of his upbringing, someone who has finally realised that he NEEDS interaction, NEEDS to feel close, NEEDS to reach out and touch, NEEDS TO NEED… and before I completely humiliate myself, let me finish with the words I said last week. I am a virgin. Be gentle with me. I leave myself in your hands. I am finally open to change, and that is the singularly most surprising, life altering thing I have ever said."

He sat.

"Well, Max. Well, well, well. And your 'well', metaphorically speaking, is flowing over. Your dam has burst, your arms are unfolded, and your mind is open enough to set your heart free. Welcome to the world. I don't think I need to add anything, your words said it all. God bless you, and painful though it may be, welcome on board.

"Well done class. Well done indeed. I am impressed, and I may add, more than a little touched. You have your assignment: 'What Is Love?' Off you go, let the healing begin.

"Class dismissed."

As they filed out, nobody was in such a hurry as last week to rush off to their own little haven. Instead they lingered, talking and exchanging thoughts. Everyone was buzzing.

Penelope turned to Lillie, who was standing on her left. "So, Lillie, hi properly, nice to meet you. Boy, it's been interesting so far, hasn't it? I certainly had no idea that all these exposés on this express train would be happening, did you? I mean, I just wanted to study psychology. What about you?"

"Yes, it is nice to meet you, Penelope. You took the words out of my mouth. Exactly what I was thinking as we left class today. I mean, I don't mind what's going on, but I do wonder what the result will be. And I do get the feeling that this direction was not exactly what the professor had in mind. I get the feeling that *this*, whatever it is, just happened, and he is going with the flow. And I do like him. I even find him quite sexy… whoops, didn't mean to say that. It just slipped out."

"Well, thank you for the validation, Lillie. And shouldn't you say it just 'Freudianly' slipped out, because I noticed a spark between you two. Me being the excellent people reader I am. It was hard to miss. I think he finds you, shall we say, unfathomable! I mean, I know we don't know each other properly or for very long, but I do want to say, just for the record, I think there is something there. Most definitely."

Lillie blushed, which she did not do easily, looked down at her shoes, played with her hooped earrings, juggled the papers in her arms, and said," Wow, that's a mouthful, I will ponder on that!" then made her excuses and left. "Bye for now. See you at the next class. And again, good to meet you," she said, quickly striding away.

Peter was standing apart from the rest of the students, but close enough to hear that conversation. He felt a little let down, as if he was honest, he was kind of hoping that he and Lillie could get something romantic going. Well, for Christ's sake, he thought, the professor is a much older man; surely I am still in with a chance. Okay, time to put on the charm. And with that thought he said his goodbyes to his classmates and strode purposefully towards his dormitory. "I need a plan," he said aloud to nobody.

Max, Edmund, Patricia and Penelope were left standing together. A little uncomfortably because friendships had not yet been properly established.

"How about we all go for a quick drink? I don't know about you, but I could do with a little light relief," Edmund said to the three of them. "First round's on me."

A collective yes went up and they started down the sidewalk for the short walk to the student bar.

Edmund led the way, next to Penelope, with Max and Patricia just behind.

"So, Penelope, hi to you, good to have you in class. In fact, just 'perfect'. Oh my God, you must get so sick of that, sorry! How are you enjoying this course so far?" Without waiting for a response, he continued, "I am enjoying it very much. It really is making me stop and think about what has happened in my life, and how it has affected the grown up I am now. I don't think I have ever spent so much time on 'me 'and I must say, I am enjoying the journey. It is a little frightening at times because we are all being so open, and again, I have never been so open in my life. Oh my God, I am babbling. So, how do you like the course so far?"

"Hi Edmund, how are you doing. Hmm, that's a good question, not sure if I have the answer to that yet. I am certainly finding it challenging. And I find myself wondering at my actual reasons for signing up for this course, and I think the reason is 'me'. And that's okay. I am happy to run naked through this emotional maze, and see where it takes me, and hope to go streaking towards the finish line."

They continued to walk to the bar, as the conversation behind them flowed.

"Hi Patricia," Max said, putting his hand out to shake. "How are ya... good to meet ya.

"You know, when you were telling your story today, as closed as I am, I could relate to it, but from the pessimistic side, of course..." He smiled sardonically. "Indeed, pain can be a comfort, and we all hold on to it because it is familiar. Oh yes. I know what this is, here it comes again, just like I expected... the difference is, if you don't mind my saying, I don't, or at least try not to repeat the pattern. You seem to have the opposite problem and always repeat the pattern. Anyway, hope I am not prying, I just found what you said today very interesting."

"Hi Max, no problem whatsoever. As I said, my heart remains on my sleeve, and that is a habit I can't break. I also enjoyed your story, very much. But - and this is just my humble opinion - don't you actually repeat your pattern of not repeating your pattern all the time? It's the same thing, isn't it? I go into the bad relationship, you pre think it, and avoid it... same problem, same thing, albeit from different sides of the equation. So maybe we are both in same boat."

Finally reaching the bar, they joined the crowded, loud, smoky filled atmosphere and for the first time that day, all started to relax.

Later that evening…

Penelope sat at the small desk in her room, with a large pad of paper and pencil, and her trusty typewriter, clean paper ready to be inserted, to begin her homework. She was a touch typer, able to get the words on the page with speed, but this was not a fast assignment. This would take some careful consideration. "In fact," she said aloud, "I should not be typing this at all, I should be writing in out longhand." She went to the small couch, took off her shoes and tucked her feet into the cushion. "Okay… here we go."

Ten Reasons to be Afraid by Penelope Perfect. About one hour later, she had her list finished.

"Make of that what you will, classmates and Professor Handover. And tomorrow I will tackle 'What Is Love'. Gee, that should be fun," she said to the walls, turned off the light and climbed into bed.

Max was lying on his bed; sleep would not come. He was thinking and thinking and thinking. I find Patricia very appealing in a 'victim 'kind of way. I wonder why that is. I am usually attracted to strong women who don't fall to pieces when it's all over, and she is certainly not that. Penelope is much more my type. She hates clingy, and always likes the exit clearly marked, which is exactly like me… so why in God's name am I attracted to Patricia? I have never felt this kind of uneasiness before. Could it be that I am afraid of hurting her? Am I afraid of being just another man who breaks her heart? Or am I afraid of caring for somebody at all? Good questions, eh Max, he thought to himself. Okay. Let's get started on the essay. He too preferred to write longhand, so he got his favourite ballpoint pen and a large yellow pad of paper, sat on his couch and began.

'What Is Love' by Max Morose.

Love is a many splintered thing… Great beginning, eh?

Edmund ambled around his room, doing a little tidying up, washing a few cups and saucers, wiping the surface where he had spilled some sugar, switching on the radio for a millisecond then switching it off again, and finally deciding to tackle the essay. Blank piece of paper, pencil with eraser poised, ready to go.

'What is love' by Edmund P Woodhouse Jr.

Love is an emotion which we have no control over, 'control 'being the operative word. I guess what I mean is L.O.V.E. is a loss of control, which can be a very frightening situation to find yourself in; it requires a leap of faith...

And he was off and running.

Peter had a restless night; sleep did not come easy. He was thinking about the conversation he had overheard between Lillie and Penelope. He liked Lillie a lot.

Even though they barely knew each other, it didn't matter. He was attracted to her. Coming from a non-communicating family, he was finding it hard to verbalise his emotions even to himself, alone in his room. God, I do hope the professor and Lillie don't get something going, damn and damn again. Maybe I should make my intentions known somehow. That's it. After the next class is over, I will start my campaign of wooing. Decision made. And now: the essay.

Peter began to type on the clunky old typewriter that he was reluctant to ever get rid of, since it had got him through so much of his school days. And his handwriting was atrocious.

As he was composing, a surprising thought edged its way into the corner of his mind, literally out of left field. And in this new 'searching for answers 'frame of mind, he let it properly come into focus. He had felt it before, but always pushed it away. Why did he always go for the unobtainable? Could it be that he didn't want it to happen at all, could it be that perhaps he preferred men? God knows where that thought flew in from. Never questioned my sexuality before, he thought. Put that in your pipe and smoke it - an old-fashioned phrase his father often used, which stuck like glue in his memory. Wow. Okay. Here I go.

Lillie ambled around for a couple of days, no direction known. Her thoughts were all over the place, not sharp and focused as they usually were. She was thinking about the professor. She knew he liked her, like any woman does... instinct, can't beat it. But. How did she feel? Was this a road she wanted to go down? Was this a road to disaster, heartbreak, exposed and naked? My

74

God, girl. Just perfect. Fall for your psychology teacher. Oh yeah. Here we go!

Finally on the third day, she settled down and began her take on 'What is Love'.

Patricia had allowed Max to see her to her dormitory front door. He didn't ask for permission, he just walked with her. But she was old fashioned, and this is how she saw it. He escorted her, like a gentleman should do. She found herself thinking about him off and on for the rest of the evening. "Oh God," she whispered to the walls, "Not again! I mustn't fall for the most unobtainable, emotionally deficient man in the class. I may as well save myself the trouble and slit my wrists now!"

Okay, this seemed to be a perfect point to begin this week's assignment…

So, Patricia, she said to herself, give yourself a big hug, and jump in with both feet. She started to write.

Autumn was in full swing on campus, and just like the song says, the hallowed halls of ivy never looked more beautiful. The six students kept mainly to themselves that week, but did bump into each other having coffee, or a quick pint of beer at the student bar. Most of it was unplanned, except for Peter, who ambled from café to bar and back again trying to run into Lillie to begin his seduction campaign. He finally succeeded early Sunday evening, and caught her sitting on a bar stool, sipping a glass of white wine, all alone, deep in thought. Perfect, he thought, and tapped her on the shoulder.

"Oh, hi Peter. Good to see you," she purred, looking very sexy yet unattainable. "Why not take a load off and have a glass with me, you look like you could do with a little pick me up."

Peter sat on the empty stool next to her - thinking, boy, that's lucky - ordered a Scotch and coke, cleared his throat several times, looked around the pub at who else was there, and tried to find a place to begin the conversation… any conversation. Jesus, he was tongue-tied. Shit. Okay. Here I go.

"How did you do with your essay? I found mine hard going at first, but finally got it done through a process of elimination, believe it or not." He laughed softly. "I am all ready for the next class and quite happy with my little piece.

"Actually, Lillie, just curious, what do you make of the professor? Do you like him?" Even as he spoke, he wondered if he was making a tactical error.

He took a sip of his drink and waited for the reply, daring to look directly into her beautiful hazel eyes. He hoped his eyes were conveying his interest and not his desperation.

"Well, Peter, funny you should ask. First, do I like him. Yes, I guess I do.

"He is intelligent, humorous, if you like that kind of humour, and just a little sad inside.

"There is a lot more to him than meets the eye. And not bad on the eyes either. I would say he is like a good book that you have to read carefully so you don't miss anything... What about you; what's your take on the teacher?"

"Yeah, I guess I like him too. He seems to 'get 'people quickly. He seems to go right past facades and look straight through everyone, which I suppose makes him a good teacher, and the right teacher for the six of us. He certainly knows how to push buttons. I wonder how old he is. Must be fifty at least. An only child, never married, not in a relationship, no children, in fact his teaching seems to be all he has.

"I feel kind of sorry for him."

They finished their drinks and enjoyed some small talk about various subjects. Peter managed to rest his arm on her shoulder - just friendly, mind you - and she did not shrug it off. Step one accomplished. I may be in with a chance here, he thought to himself, and I will drop into the conversation the professor's age at every available opportunity. Drinks over, they said goodnight; after all, tomorrow was a school day.

Class 5

Clapping his hands together, Professor Handover welcomed his six pupils.

"Let's jump right in, shall we? I have been looking forward all week to today.

"You all certainly had a lot to think about. I did too. Okay, before we get to your individual essays, Penelope, please stand up and share with us your extra assignment. I await with baited ears." He chuckled, and winked at Lillie, which Peter caught.

Penelope looked pretty, dressed in a blue denim dress with a white lace collar, paired with white Doc Martens, managing to look tough and vulnerable at the same time.

"Okay, here it goes." She cleared her throat, which didn't need clearing, and began.

Ten Reasons to be Afraid, by Penelope Perfect

1. Finding someone attractive who doesn't find me attractive equals rejection.

2. Somebody finding me attractive, but not reciprocated, equals second hand rejection, which is somehow worse!

3. Somebody finding my conversation lacking equals subjective.

4. Somebody not laughing at my razor-sharp wit equals ego deflation.

5. Somebody falling in love with me too hard and too needy equals suffocation.

6. Me falling in love too hard and losing myself completely equals dehumanisation.

7. Somebody breaking up with me first equals humiliation.

8. Me breaking up with somebody and finding out I was wrong equals damnation.

9. Falling in love, hoping it would complete my puzzle equals delusion.

10. Finding out that contrary to romantic illusion, I am better off alone, which equals confusion.

She gazed around the room slowly, looking at each of her classmates and the professor carefully, reading them, as she always did, but also aware that they were reading her.

"Do any of you have any comments on Penelope's list?"

Patricia raised her hand.

"Yes, my dear, go ahead."

"Well, I was making notes as you were reading your list, Penelope, and interestingly, this is my list, from your list, a recap if you like.

"1, rejection, 2, second hand rejection, 3, subjective, 4, ego deflation, 5, suffocation, 6, dehumanisation, 7, humiliation, 8, damnation, 9, delusional, and 10, illusion equals confusion. Seems to me that beneath that 'optimistic 'exterior beats a pessimistic heart."

"Interesting, Patricia; I must say my thoughts were heading in the same direction. Penelope, do you agree with what's been said?"

"It has certainly given me food for thought. I never looked at myself that way, and it does feel like there may be some truth to it. If you don't mind, I would prefer to leave my list alone now so I can digest properly… to be continued when I have figured a few things out, if that's okay."

"Certainly, and I agree, do digest, take as much time as you need."

"Thank you, and now I will read the essay I have prepared."

What Is Love?

Many have tried to explain this word, many have failed. There are so many different kinds of love, but let's take romantic love for the sake of argument. You meet, you like the look and feel of someone, you get little stabs of pleasure looking at them, kissing them, just holding hands gives you a jolt. Now, it could be argued that this is lust, not love... so, what's the difference between the two?

Lust is an uncontrollable urge to possess, to dominate, it's unexplainable and non-negotiable, you feel out of control, which to me is delicious. Until of course that lust is satisfied, and then it slips out of you as quickly as it appeared (pun intended), leaving you sexually satisfied but strangely empty inside.

So, what is love? Let's examine the similarities, first.

Like lust, love is also uncontrollable, with the same urge to possess.

But there are key differences.

Love is not 'out of control' – or shouldn't be, anyway.

Love embraces jealousy fondly, which lust has no time for.

And, whereas lust leaves you sexually satisfied but empty, love leaves your heart satisfied and fills you up inside. And if it is true love, the feeling stays forever. So, I am told, if all the sonnets and songs are to believed, love makes the world go round, blah blah blah...

So, what is love?

Well, it's a four-letter word that I certainly have not experienced in my life. Lust is also a four-letter word, and believe me, been there, done that, many times.

Maybe the answer is very simple.

What is love?

Love is not being afraid to love.

Cue the violins.

The End.

Spontaneous applause broke out amongst her classmates and the professor, with a few cheers thrown in for good measure.

"Does anyone have anything to ask, or to add to Ms. Perfect's essay?"

Patricia raised her hand again.

"Can I ask, Penelope, have you never even been close to being in love; you know, a too close encounter? There must have been at least one guy who managed to run down your inside track. I am curious."

"That's a good question, and the fact that I am not hesitating is your answer. Of course I have been close, and I ran for the hills, scared the shit – sorry – the bejesus out of me. I am just not comfortable with these kinds of feelings. And I can only be who I am. Whether or not I find that there is a loving lover of falling in love, trying to get out, we shall see. But until it happens, I am what I am."

"Okay, let's have a male point of view now and even things up."

Looking around the room, the professor said, "Okay Edmund, you're up."

What Is Love? By Edmund P Woodhouse Jr.

Love, in my opinion, is an emotion which we have no control over, and I mean *no control* over, which can be a very frightening situation to find yourself in, especially if you are a control freak like me. To fall requires a leap of faith in the dark. Nobody really understands it, and very few people get out alive. I have taken that leap more than once, and have survived, and will probably fall again when the opportunity presents itself. But I want to focus on parental love, not romantic. This is an entirely different kind of love. If you are born into a family, some say we choose, and maybe we do, anyway… you meet your mother and father, who in my case is not my father. During my formative years, I eavesdropped and found out the truth, and this fact changed my feelings for both my mother and my father. It poses the question, is love automatic between child and parents, and if it is automatic, can it be destroyed or does nature dictate the outcome? Do we have any control over these feelings? Is it possible to not love your parents, and if you don't love them, does this make you an evil person?

I think that love is subjective, and I prefer to observe love in all its forms from an emotional distance. And I prefer to question its validity.

I will end with this

Love Is …………. You can add an adjective of your own choice.

"Thank you, Edmund. It seems to me we are redefining our original proclamations from class one. Penelope seems to be a closet pessimist. And you do too, I might say. Interesting. Okay. Who's next? Patricia?"

"Okay, here we go, I have decided to write a fictional piece for my essay and a little poem thrown in at the end for good measure."

What Is Love? By Patricia Hodges
She was walking through the school corridors one afternoon, aimlessly, nowhere in particular to go, when her eyes rested on a perfect specimen of manhood. A not-allowed leather jacket over his school blazer, God, that must be hot, chewing gum with his slightly too long sideburns and a sexy sneer, leaning on his locker looking, necktie askew. There she was in her boring school skirt, rolled up to make it shorter, boring white blouse, and boring sensible shoes. God, she hated these uniforms.

"How ya doing there, honey? What's your name? Mine's Randy. And you sure are a pretty little thing."

Blushing sweetly, she replied, "Hi there, I am Allison" (thinking to herself, you sure are a a good-looking guy).
And now my poem.
Boy meets girl, romance and bliss.
They fall in love,
and then he falls out.
Boy leaves girl, it ends amiss.
What is love,
if it starts with a kiss.
What is love?
It's hit and miss.
The End

A collective "awwwwww" rumbled around the classroom, even from Max, who was thinking to himself how much he liked this girl, her innocence, her sweetness, and most of all, her vulnerability. Oh boy, tread carefully, these are uncharted waters for you.

"Max, your turn."

"Okay… here's mine."

What Is Love? By Max Morose.

Love is a 'many splintered thing, '(He paused for effect) mainly because you get nailed to the cross, and your emotions get hung out to dry. It's heaven and hell. And they *can* exist simultaneously. It's a kind of torture. It's an emotion I have never trusted because it means opening yourself up to another. I never wanted to do that. But even though I never trusted LOVE, I decided many years ago that I would, however, allow myself to fall in love and I did in fact fall in love, deeply, and conducted the love affair of all time… but…

The love affair was with myself.

And *that's* what true love is.

Amen to that.

"Thank you, Max, and congratulations, you remain a pessimist. Long may your love affair continue, and a word of caution, make sure you don't try and run away from yourself, because you can't." The professor chuckled.

Patricia and Max exchanged a small glance, which Penelope caught, which made her think. She read their silent conversation the following way: Max's I is slipping, he likes her, likes her a lot, and Patricia is just plain scared, which I would be too with her past record. Very interesting, I will be watching this develop, which I am sure it will, even though I kind of like Max myself, and damn, I thought it was reciprocated. Over and out.

"Now let's see, just two of you left, okay Peter."

What Is Love? By Peter Pendergast

I have approached this assignment from the other side, so instead of, what IS love, I have written what love ISN'T; by process of elimination I have come to my conclusion.

Love isn't a chemical reaction

Love isn't mistrust

Love isn't envy

Love isn't predictable

Love isn't easy

Love isn't free
Love is not for sale
Love isn't hiding
Love isn't a battle
So, what is love?
Love is confusing because,
Love just may be all the above.
I will end this with a question
Is love, what love isn't?
How's that for sidestepping the issue?

"Thank you, Peter, and now finally, the exotic Lillie Lawford."

What Is Love? By Lillie Lawford
    This was not a subject that came easy for me to write about; having been emotionally cocooned for most of my life I have forced myself to delve down into the dreaded L word. It is an attraction, both physical and mental. We have all had this experience. It is that uncomfortable moment when you realise, hey, I like this person, and immediately, well for me anyway, I back up into the corner I've always hidden in, but in my defence, even when I hide, I am in full view. But I digress.
    I do believe in love, one hundred per cent; whether it will happen to me as they write about in the romantic stories, I have my doubts. What is love? For me it is simply declaring to myself, and to my classmates, I am open to persuasion. I think I should wear a sign on my back: danger, deep waters. And who knows, maybe I will sink before I even learn how to swim.
    The End

Lillie finished, and looked slowly at each of her classmates, mystery shining out of her eyes, and hesitating just that moment too long on the professor.
    Was he blushing?
    He was.
    "Excellent, well done. I am impressed with each one of your essays.

83

"In our next class we will be studying action versus reaction. What our personal flashpoints are. Why we have these buttons that are so easily pushed, and if they are harmful to us. What gets your goat, is it uncontrollable, where did it come from, and how do we get rid of it? Off you go and think about it. I want a list from everyone for our next class, which we will read, act out, and then discuss. Now don't forget, there will be another class on Thursday. From here on in we will meet twice a week instead of once. So you only have a couple of days to do your homework. Class dismissed."

Everyone filed out slowly, and a few comments were exchanged on the way. Lillie held back until the room had emptied, without making it obvious. The professor was sitting at his desk looking down at his notes for the day, until, finally feeling there was someone still in the room, he looked up and was pleased to see who it was.

"Yes, Lillie, did you have a question about something?"

"Yes, Professor, would you like to go for a quick drink with me? There are a few things I would like to pick your brain about."

"Splendid, my dear, I'll just grab my coat and hat."

The exotic student and the stern-looking professor linked arms in the proper way for a gentleman and a lady walking along the pathways, as he walked her to a bar in town, not the campus one. Lillie realised it but did not say a word. She was glad. No questions asked!

It was a beautiful autumn night, not too cold, and the leaves were gathering in all their hues, on the ground, crunching and crackling under their feet, as they strolled along the sidewalk. Both were content to be silent and just enjoy the peaceful mood. They seemed to be perfectly in tune.

They entered a dimly lit bar called Angelo's, which also served snacks, found a quiet table, and sat down. There was a nice fire going, and the atmosphere was very cosy.

They both ordered a nice cold glass of Chardonnay and finally, they talked.

Lillie began,

"So, Professor, I just needed to have a little private time with you to clarify things. I won't beat around the bush. I find you

84

very attractive, and if my instinct is correct, the feeling is returned. And I still won't beat around the bush: there is a big age difference, which gives me pause. Okay. Your turn."

"Well, Ms. Lawford, you certainly don't waste any time do you?! And please, out of school hours, do call me Friedrich, and if I may, I will call you Lillie.'

"Works for me," Lillie replied.

"Now, if I am reading you correctly, you are trying to decide whether to proceed with this little flirtation. Where is it going? Where can it go? And you are probably just a little scared because, after all, I am the psychology teacher, and maybe you will not be able to hide from me, and hiding is something you have managed your entire life… so far! Have I got that correct?"

"Yep, a hundred per cent. Okay, ah… Friedrich. To be honest, when I wrote my essay, I focused on you. Yes, it makes me nervous, of course, how could it not? I mean, my God, this could turn into a real mind fuck. Whoops, sorry, that just slipped out."

The professor chucked softly to himself. He liked this girl very much.

"I am guessing you must be around fifty, and I am mere twenty-one… that's a huge age gap. I would like to know *why* you find me attractive, I mean, what draws you to me. I am trying to understand what's happening here. I don't know, maybe verbalising it is not the way forward, but I am not comfortable just 'feeling 'it, so, I need it laid out in black and white. I need answers, so… what's the score? Why me?"

The professor, as his maturity allowed, took his time answering, looking at her face, enjoying her discomfort, and falling into her eyes. He was in no hurry and did not want to ruin this moment. Truth be told, this was a moment he had never experienced before, and he was surprised how quickly it was happening, and how well he was handling it. Hmm, he thought, I guess I have been waiting all my life for something like this to happen, I just never knew it.

"Well, Lillie, you have asked fair questions, and I will be honest with you. I like that you are unreachable, in a cool kind of way, yet the dichotomy is, I find you very, very warm, in a 'touchable 'way. Basically, I feel like I can see right through into your core. I love the armour you wear, and would love to unlock it, bit by bit. I feel like we are kindred souls, and these are uncharted seas for both of us, as you said in your essay today. And to be honest, I did feel it was aimed in my direction. The sentence I liked most was, 'I am open to persuasion.' So, if you are... Shall we dance?"

"Yes, Friedrich, as long as I can choose the music."

And the flirtation between student and teacher was off and running.

Max and Patricia, Penelope and Edmund found themselves once again at the student bar, which was becoming a little bit of a habit after class, but an enjoyable one.They ordered drinks and chit-chatted about today's class. They were becoming comfortable with one another.

Peter had waited near the school exit doors hoping to catch Lillie as she left. Thank goodness he caught a glimpse of them leaving together and could fade into the shadows before he was seen. Damn. Looks like this is a happening situation here, he thought to himself. Well, let's not take anything for granted. It could be perfectly innocent. Let's see what I see in the next class. And, if it looks like the romance is going forward, I will simply retreat and wait for the fall out, which I am pretty sure will happen. And then I will return, the conquering hero, and sweep her into my arms. Good God, Peter, get a grip, he cautioned under his breath, and made his way dejectedly back to his room. By the time he had unlocked the front door he was standing tall again. He was a very determined boy at heart. He had had to be with his family! And he had a plan.

There were only three days until the next class, and all the students were very aware of this. They spent their time delving once again into their psyches in preparation. This was neither pleasant nor easy.

Class 6

Everyone was seated. The sun was streaming through the dusty window on the campus side, which was unusual for October, and very welcome it was. It was a big room for only six students. There was the required teacher's desk, with a pad of paper, a pen and a pencil on top, and a typewriter pushed to the side, the large blackboard with chalk and eraser, and several shelves containing various books on psychology. The room was silent, waiting for the professor to begin. Oddly, there were two extra chairs in front of his desk today, facing each other.

"Good morning class. I am going to try something a little unconventional today.

"I know you've all done your homework, and I also know that you would have found this week's assignment a little unsettling. The very nature of this subject has a negative connotation, and it usually means, something gets you angry, which none of us like, and even more, do not like to admit to. These things are a hidden deficit... only today, I am holding you all to account." He chuckled and thought, God, I am funny. "We will go in pairs today. First up, completely at random, I am going to put Peter together with Lillie. Could you both come up front and sit on the chairs? Thank you.

"Okay... Peter, off you go."

Peter got his notes out of his jacket pocket, looked them over, and began.

"Okay, one of my person problems is explaining myself, either in a group, or singular situation, quite articulately and transparently I might add, in my opinion anyway, and not being heard, or understood. This makes me livid. I feel like I have wasted my words. Even reading this right now gets me a little angry. I hate to be ignored; I hate to be misunderstood."

"Okay, thank you, and now you, Lillie."

"Right, well, what I have a problem with is jealousy, or resentment, whatever term you want to use, although jealously seems to be the nastier of the adjectives. There is a certain look, a lowering of the eyebrows, a smirk, a 'who do you think you are' caption written on someone's face, not mine I might add, and most of the time it is for no reason, which really annoys me. What the hell have I done? I am just being me. This has happened to me many times, and I do fly into a rage over it. But not publicly, oh no. I won't give them/her/him the satisfaction. I simply walk away, straight into my emotional brick wall! Is that what they call being 'stoned'? Sorry, a little levity was called for. I'm done."

"Okay, thank you both for that. Now for the experiment. Peter, I want you to look Lillie straight in the eye and tell her something that you need and want her to understand about you. Honesty is called for here on both parts. Put your egos under the chair and simply listen and react. That is all that is required."

Embarrassed silence ensued, as everyone looked at each other in confusion. What the hell was going on?

Peter cleared his throat, thought about his plan, made a silent decision, and dove right in.

"Lillie, I may seem a little frivolous to you, class clown springs to mind, but as these lessons have shown, there is much more to me than meets the eye. I have a very serious side, I am compassionate, kind and warm, and I have a lot to offer to the right woman. And I have been waiting a long time to find that woman. Do you understand me?"

Lillie looked long and hard at Peter. Wow, she thought, if this is what I think it is, damn… how do I get out of this without hurting him? Damn, if only the professor wasn't in the equation, I would have been hearing this with different ears. Okay, honesty, total, and here we go.

"Peter, I hear you loud and clear, and believe me, I *do* understand your intention. I would like to say that the right woman, whoever she is, may indeed be right for *you*, but you may be wrong for *her*. There is no guarantee that when you fall, the object of your affection will automatically follow suit and fall in love with you. Have I read you correctly?"

"Yes, it does because you are avoiding the issue, which is a hundred per cent what I am talking about. Not being understood. If you do understand me, which I believe you do, I am trying to ask you out for a date." There, he thought, I've gone and said it.

The professor leapt in quickly to save the situation.

"Okay, Peter, okay Lillie, well done... very well done. Let's save the personal requests for after class though, shall we? So, the experiment has worked. Peter, you did speak clearly, and Lillie, you either purposely or not, didn't understand him. The point is, your issue was exposed, very plainly. I am going to put it to the class, do any of you think Peter did *not* make himself clear; do you think he was speaking ambiguously, or was his message quite transparent?"

Penelope raised her hand immediately.

"Well, the way I see it is, Peter, although you seemed to have spoken quite straightforwardly and articulately, I got the feeling that you were, in fact, being ambiguous, boxing clever, hoping that Lillie would pick up the hidden - and I say hidden - message. Because of the ending, when you said, do you understand me? I would have pointed that right up so there would be no mistake and said, do *you* understand me... and then said it again: do *you* understand me. Then it would have indeed been obvious. Instead, what you did was give Lillie a chance to prevaricate, to be ambiguous back and to sidestep the question, so you were forced to declare it outright, in a rather humiliating manner. But that's just my humble opinion."

Lillie had the grace to look embarrassed. In fact, the entire class was a little subdued. Peter had indeed put his heart on his sleeve, and was not heard in the process. Not comfortable for anybody.

"Okay, thank you for taking part, Peter. Lillie, stay where you are and Penelope please come up and join us, and share with us your input for today's discussion."

Penelope tentatively came to the front of the class and sat on the chair facing a not-so-friendly-looking Lillie.

"It's funny but I seem to have perfected the art of hiding, but of course that's not going to get me off the hook here. What truly annoys me is bullshit, no other word for it, bullshit. I have a

89

thing about truth, no matter how uncomfortable. I don't want it dressed up, I don't want it disguised, I want it straight up and on the table, so I can deal with it properly. I guess the worst scenario, which has happened to me many times, is let's say family get into an argument. Now of course every person will have their perception of said argument, but, as I have always maintained, facts are facts, perception is perception. Two different things.

"The many times I have had to lay down the law of what happened to family members who coloured the situation their own way, I really hate that. And I can be quite fierce. I once threatened to throw my little sister out the ground floor window if she did not tell the truth about something that had happened. She told the truth. I have always said, I would rather be hurt with the truth than misled with a lie."

"Lillie, do you have a comment for Penelope?"

"Yes, I do. Penelope, *your* truth is not necessarily *their* truth, and in my experience, the truth is always somewhere in the middle. Do you think it's possible, while the facts are rolling out, that you can misinterpret them, and therefore make your truth out to be the actual truth? I know it seems convoluted, but I know what I mean. Yes, facts are facts, yes perception is perception, but at some point, they do intersect? You know that old game of getting in a circle, whispering something to the next person, with the instructions that they must repeat the same sentence to the next one and so on until you get to the end, and the last person must say it out loud? It is always different to the way it began. So, although you may hate bullshit, it will find its way into most situations."

The feeling between the two girls was tense now. Neither liked what the other had said.

"Lillie, I hear you, but to be honest, I find your comments to be condescending, and it feels to me like you're talking down to me like a naughty child who doesn't understand the basics of life. I resent your attitude."

"That was not my intention at all. But, hooray, there's that word. You have hit my nail on the head. I hate resentment. As I said earlier, all I am doing is being me. I would say your level of acceptance is very low, especially if anyone dares to disagree with you. You hate bullshit, so I will give you zero bullshit." She said this rather smugly.

Once again, the professor jumped in.

"Excellent, both of you. Without even trying you exposed your issues and played them out. I couldn't have scripted it better had I tried. Now shake hands, both of you, and return to your seats. Okay, Edmund and Max, please take the hot seats."

Edmund got out some notes from his blazer pocket, looking very ill at ease. Max just sat there, looking smug, and very unbothered.

"Shake hands boys, you are about to box clever... let's make it a good clean fight. Edmund, off you go."

"I found this to be a very difficult assignment, I must admit. Mainly because I'm not really a fly-off-the-handle kind of person, happy or not. And I am a little gun shy to be honest. I dug deep down and tried to find areas in my gut that do make me angry, I dug and dug and dug... and finally I found that in fact, what really does anger me is not being able to be angry. That is frustrating. I would love to blow up, to let off steam, but it seems I only simmer. So it would be good if somebody, maybe you Max, since we are in the hot seats, can find my anger. I must have hidden it a long time ago and thrown away the key. So, my trigger is I have no trigger!" He made a pistol shape with his hands, pointed it at his head, said "'Bang," and blew on the end of the gun.

"Let's throw it to the class: does anyone have an idea how we can trigger poor seemingly triggerless Edmund here?"

Silence ensued. No one took the bait.

Then Max spoke.

"I'll have a go at this, please. Edmund, when you think of your 'father, 'how does it make you feel? Do you love him? Do you? Or what about your mother, do you hate the deceit you have lived with? And when you sometimes wonder about your real father, which you must do or you wouldn't be normal, do you sometimes feel rudderless, like a boat in the middle of the sea? Do you wonder who you truly are, what your real bloodline is? Does not knowing make you feel unworthy?"

Edmund sat there a minute with no expression on his face, his arms stiff at his sides, fists clenched, and suddenly leapt up, knocking the chair over in the process, and punched Max on the chin, knocking him off his chair.

Edmund, anger spent, then offered his hand to Max and helped him off the floor, quietly picked up his chair, put it upright, sat back down, looking very calm, and said, "Thank you, Max, for helping me to locate my anger. I have needed to do that for a very long time, and voila, here it is." He made a gun shape again. "I shot you down."

The professor, who really should have reported this situation, which was strictly against the rules of conduct, decided to wait a few moments and see what happened next.

Max rubbed his chin, looked Edmund directly in the eye for a full two minutes, made an internal decision and said, "That's okay, buddy. Glad I could be of assistance. But be aware, next time I hit back."

"Fair enough, Max. Sorry about that."

"Edmund," the professor said rather sharply, "there will be no more of that in my classroom, is that clear?"

Pause.

"Right Max, I believe you're next."

Still rubbing his chin, Max began to speak.

"I too found this assignment difficult, only because I am the kind that keeps my true feelings very close to my chest. Safer that way. And, as you all know, I am not a pushover, except for Edmund's sucker punch. So, the only thing I can come up with where my psyche is concerned is unnecessary violence, which is amazing considering what just happened. Because I do have a history of this, with my own father, I cannot bear to see it happen to anyone else, especially a youngster, I see red, and fly into a rage. I would say, I become dangerous. The good thing is, I know this can happen, I accept the reason why and I try very hard to not let it get the better of me. Knowing your triggers, that's important; you can't fix 'em, at least I don't think you can, but you can change how you react to them. Also, if I am being very honest, again because of my upbringing, I despise vulnerability. It destroyed my mother. She should have had more balls. So, two triggers for the price of one, both as a direct result of my parents. I think I deserve a gold star."

"Once again, I ask the class, does anyone have a comment?" A hand went up. "Yes, Patricia?"

"My question to you, Max, is the following. If your mother had more balls, as you so eloquently put it, she wouldn't be your mother, at least not the mother you know and love, despite what you say. And may I be so bold as to suggest that the reason you find her vulnerability so annoying is, to my eyes anyway, not annoying at all, simply too close to home. You are your mother's son. I see you, beneath that ultra cool, unapproachable persona, as a very vulnerable young man, who I find quite appealing."

"Okay, let me stop you there. Edmund, you may go back to your seat. Patricia, come and join us."

She did.

"Max, do you have anything to say regarding Patricia's observation?"

"Well, I have promised myself that I will try very hard to be open in this class, so this is me trying very hard! Yes, you nailed it. And to be perfectly honest, I am now angry at myself for being vulnerable. Congratulations. My mojo is exposed."

"Okay Patricia, you are our final speaker... off you go."

"Well, like everyone else in this class, my problems are a direct result of my life so far. Because of my low batting average with men, I am prone to jealousy when I see a pretty woman, which angers me because it is so stupid, and I know it and so beneath me... but it does happen. I immediately compare my looks with hers and wonder, am I good enough, then berate myself for even going there. Jealousy is such an ugly, damaging thing.

"It is there all the time. I *would* like to get rid of it."

Max turned to her, asking, "Patricia, how about you try to approach it another way? When you feel this coming on, twist it round. Say to yourself, wow, this girl is pretty, in fact, say it to the girl herself. Give a compliment. Watch her face light up, watch her smile. You will feel good about it. Don't let someone else's good looks become your deficit.

"And, can I add, you look adorable to me."

They locked eyes, experiment over.

"Thank you everyone. That was very interesting... very. And I think that concludes the lessons for today. Next week is an off week, so can I suggest you all relax and enjoy yourselves. No homework."

The class filed out silently, with lots to think about. Once outside the school doors, Peter broke the mood. "Hey guys, let's all get together for a party. After all, no assignment was given so why not?"

A general murmur of agreement from all.

"Where shall we have it?" said Max.

Edmund piped up, "How about we book that nice pizza place in town, make it a meal, some wine and conversation. If we're going to do it let's do it properly."

Everyone agreed it was a good plan.

Penelope added, "Okay, great, I will phone the restaurant and book us in, six people for six p.m., on the sixth, which is in three days. See you there."

After various goodbyes, they all walked their separate ways back to their digs.

The sixth arrived without a sound as all six students arrived at the pizza place pretty much at the same time. Everyone had on their Sunday best. Everyone looked good and everyone knew it. Let the festivities begin.

Chairs were pulled out randomly; no one seemed to care much about who they were sitting next to. Thank goodness it was a round table. It ended up with Max in between Penelope and Patricia, Peter next to Lillie, and Edmund on the other side of Lillie. They all quickly scanned their menus, deciding to share two very large pizzas with everything on. Two bottles of Chianti were brought to the table, uncorked and poured, and the evening began.

Peter stood up, raising his glass, and said, "I propose a toast to us, the fearless six. We all got on this ride together, and we will all get off this ride together. Where it's all heading, who knows? Anyway, cheers to all of you."

Cheers… a clinking of glasses together and they were off and running.

Max turned to Penelope. "So, how's it hanging? We haven't had a chance to talk again properly, not since our little soiree in the bar and that was weeks ago. What do you think of the course so far?"

"Well, Max, I go back and forth between loving it and hating it. Haven't made up my mind yet. It is interesting… very; and very, as the professor says, exposing…never thought I would be baring my soul like I have been doing. Not just me, all of us. Not even sure if that's what I secretly signed up for. I sure am learning a lot about me. Which is strange, because I thought all my life that the one thing I did know was, in fact, me! So, same question back to you. Without the 'how's it hanging 'bit. Not something I need to know hahaha."

She had the grace to blush, which she did often and easily. Part of her charm; even more so because she didn't realise it was part of her charm.

"How do I feel about it, now there's a question. I don't have a love/hate thing going like yours at all. What I do have going is this uncomfortable feeling. It's constant. I feel like I am in over my head, and yet for the first time that I can remember, I am not afraid of the feeling. Something inside me has shifted, not disappeared you understand, just shifted. I for one am happy to be here…. Cheers to you."

Patricia turned to the two of them and held her glass up for a cheers. "Couldn't help but overhear your conversation so hope you don't mind me putting my two cents' worth in. It sure is a hell of a course, isn't it? You both, in my opinion, come from a place of great personal strength, which is why you are both uncomfortable in your own ways with the exposés. I come from a place of great vulnerability and expect to feel uncomfortable… been uncomfortable all my life really. Nothing new there. I guess what I am trying to say is: I am hoping to shake hands with myself. I know deep down I have balls; I just need to locate them!"

Max turned to Patricia, slightly blocking Penelope, casually put his arm on the back of her chair and said quietly, "You also come from a position of strength. The strength to admit your weaknesses, that's true strength. And, possessing a cast iron set of balls myself, believe me, it's overrated."

They smiled at each other, genuine and a little flirtatious on both sides. Penelope saw it all.

All around the round table, conversation was flowing, the wine was being drunk, the two pizzas had arrived, and they all dug in, eating, drinking, laughing, enjoying, just as the professor wanted them to do.

Peter took a messy bite of his slice, and wiped his mouth, throwing himself at Lillie. He was a glass or two of wine in, so he felt foolhardy and brave, inhibitions gone.

"Lillie, I am just going to get straight to the point. You must realise that I like you, and I mean, I really like you. Forgive me for being so blunt, I blame the alcohol." Then he blurted it out: "Would you like to go out on a date with me? That is, if you are not seeing anyone else."

Lillie nibbled her pizza, playing for time, sipped her wine, and considered this request, as her thoughts rattled around in her mind. What's the harm? she thought. Just a date, not a marriage. But would I be playing him along? How serious is it with the professor? Considering the age difference, whatever happens, there will be a start and then an end. Finally she replied:" Okay, Peter. Next week would be fine. Give me a call."

Edmund sat there quietly, not engaging, just listening. He liked to do that, liked being a fly on the wall. He had learned how to not be there very young and could escape into himself quite easily. No pressure. In fact, which was a little worrying, if he allowed himself to think about it… nobody really seemed to notice that he wasn't joining in. And again, there's that old Edmund, non-reaction, leading the way. He ate his pizza and sipped his wine for the remainder of the evening. And nobody noticed all night long. Somewhere deep inside, Edmund realised he did not like being ignored, not at all. This was quite a revelation. "Cheers to me," he said quietly to himself. And again, nobody noticed… oh well.

Professor Handover deliberated between calling Lillie for a date or not. He couldn't decide, and rather than do something wrong, he did nothing. It was a long, lonely week.

Class 7

"Good afternoon, boys and girls. Hope you had a nice week off. Now, there was no assignment given, so today I thought we could all discuss what we think psychology is, our own personal opinions, Freudian or whatever, the field of interpretation is wide open. I didn't want you to have time to prepare your answers."

Looking slowly around the classroom, he pointed to Edmund." You first."

Edmund stood.

"What is psychology? Well, I believe it explains the reasons we all do as we do. I believe every little part of our personality, good and bad, has a point of origin, a reason for existing, and without making it an emotion, it becomes a scientific explanation instead, something we can all wrap our brains around and try to make sense of. It is the voice of rationality and logic, versus the screaming of our egos and personalities."

"Interesting, Edmund. Thank you. Lillie, your turn."

"I kind of agree with Edmund, with a slightly different twist to it. I too think it is the voice of reason against our egos. I approach it as a series of facts and explanations, used to illustrate all the confusion we carry around inside. Unlocking the psyche is the only way to go, it's limitless, it's scary, and hopefully it will show me the way to me. Been carrying this map for a long time. But unfortunately, I am crap at reading them."

Penelope, without being asked, stood up and began, "Funny, Professor, we all had a dinner last week, and this is one of the things I discussed with Max, in a roundabout way. We were talking about what we both think of this course. So, in my humble opinion, psychology is not for the weak minded, oh no. It takes great strength to do a biopsy of your character. My God, what you might find in the process. I think psychology is like being a detective. All the clues are there, you just must find them, put them together, and find the murderer. Whoops! Now there's a Freudian slip if there ever was one. Not even sure I answered the question, but too late to retract it now, it's already out there."

She sat.

"Who do we have left? Let's see, Peter, Patricia and Max… and which of you wants to speak next? Come on. Time is wasting," said the professor.

Patricia arose from her seat slowly.

"Well, I do tend to live in the heart more than the mind, which makes this kind of course quite difficult for me because it's all about reasons, cause and effect, mind over matter, logic, thinking things through, finding the correct answers, the correct routes to take, dissecting your past and finding triggers, digging them up and analysing them. Basically bypassing the heart in the process, which is a real conundrum, because I just don't know how that is possible. But on this course I am, and I will do my very best to try and approach 'me 'from a totally different perspective. Psychology, for me, means finding the answers to me, if that makes sense."

She sat.

Max jumped in quickly, wanting to snowball on what Patricia had said.

"Yes, I agree. It is all about analysing, dissecting, exploring, and being brave enough to dig down into the deepest part of yourself. All in the name of mental science!

"I do believe that problems we find difficult to deal with in our own personalities can all be traced back to our childhood, when our minds and emotions are like sponges and everything goes inside and stays there until we take a course like this one, and open the door on our secret corners. Some prefer to stay asleep, and some prefer to take that leap in the dark. And that's how I would describe psychology. Taking a leap in the dark. It's a toss-up for me. Am I more scared or more curious? Anyway, whatever the case, I'm jumping… without a parachute."

He sat.

Peter, the last contender, took a pregnant pause before he stood up.

"Let's see. What do I think psychology is. Well, it's an end to a means for me. Growing up in a family where nobody really communicated, this is like a smorgasbord… and boy, am I hungry for some answers. This course gives us all the opportunity to ask the questions we have always been afraid to ask. In fact, to ask questions full stop. I do slightly disagree with Patricia in one respect. I don't think this course necessarily has to bypass the heart, in fact I believe the heart of the course *is* how we feel… which of COURSE during the COURSE, of COURSE, we will find a way to explain how and why we feel how we feel. Of COURSE! Bring it on and let the healing begin."

Peter sat.

"Well done everyone, well done. We seem to have covered a lot of ground in a very short time. I would like to tell you what I think psychology is. And, since I am the professor, you should all listen with both ears, mind and heart completely open. It's not straightforward, in fact it's a very long, winding, rocky road to get to the truth.

"We are all products of our environment, the good and the bad. When we are hurt as a child, it doesn't really matter if what happened did indeed happen. How we remember it is the important part because it is our perception of said incident - that's what sticks. And this is where psychology comes in, to provide us with the way to understand the situation in a non-emotional, grown-up way. Try to be objective, which is the hardest part when you're dealing with yourself and your loved ones.

"Here's a little story about a seven-year-old boy, the same boy who I talked about quite a few classes ago when we were discussing our childhood. Now this boy has seen his parents argue and fight and witnessed the violence that would ensue since the age of five, at least that's how far back he can remember… but somehow, they were still together. He was once again witnessing his mother and father having an argument, a serious one, again, in which voices were raised, and threats were made. One step away from fists flying. Having witnessed these arguments for ever he now knew what to expect. These fights played havoc with his emotions… there is a split loyalty, there is fear of abandonment, of maybe having to choose between them, a fear of his father

99

physically hurting his mother again, yet wanting them to stay together because they are after all his mom and dad... all sorts of mixed emotions affecting his relationship with his parents, with himself, his safety, and how he conceives love, if there is such a thing. This time, the child was asked by his mother to go upstairs and bring her suitcase down, 'because I am leaving your father.' Can you imagine how he felt going up those stairs, step by step, finding the right case and reluctantly bringing it downstairs, tears falling down his face, carrying it into the room, placing it on the floor, standing there waiting for the next instruction, and then being asked to leave the two of them alone so they can talk? Can you imagine?!"

The professor stood there, oblivious to the class, for a good three minutes. Nobody moved and nobody spoke.

"And that is why I became a teacher of psychology. Class dismissed."

The professor sat lost in his memories, and the class filed out silently.

They were all immersed in the exposé Professor Handover had just displayed. All of them were lost in the enormity of what had just happened. It felt like this entire course had indeed turned course, or even coarse... and was taking them all, including the professor, into uncharted waters without so much as a life vest to help if they should get into trouble. It was like a magnet pulling them all in, yet at the same time, it was as scary as shit. "What the hell is going on?" This was the question in everyone's minds, if not quite yet on their lips.

Max naturally gravitated to Penelope. They were truly connected by their completely opposite take on things, since this opposite take on things was in fact the same, just different sides of the coin. A dichotomy indeed. It drew them together in the beginning, and it still had the same power. Heads together, they began to talk in hushed tones, because for some unknown reason, they wanted their observations to be private; although, if you asked them both why they needed it to be private, neither one of them could give you a decent answer.

"So, Pen... whose point is sharp and whose aim is true... sorry, I am being glib, and I am more than a little unsettled. Are we the students, or is the professor the student and we the teachers?"

They walked slowly together, taking a left turn to a path less travelled, as the rest turned right… analogy intended.

"Okay, Max, here's the thing. Let's bottom line it shall we? We have all been drawn for whatever reason to this college course of self-discovery. We are all emotional cripples, we are all mental giants (in our own minds anyway), and we are all, each one of us, including the professor, searching for the answers. The problem is… I don't know what the actual question is; do you?"

Max stopped dead in his tracks. Penelope had no choice but to stop too. They both stood there, looking into each other's eyes, naked, questioning, and confused, needing some answers and yet afraid of the answers to this unasked question.

"Pen… I think the question is, cliché though it may be: WHO ARE WE?

"That's the only way I can say it… WHO ARE WE? WHO THE FUCK ARE WE?"

And that said it all. Neither of them had anything more to say in this face of the inescapable truth of life. It was mind blowing, it was exhilarating, it was frightening, but most of all it was the truth. WHO THE FUCK ARE WE?

"And," Penelope added softly, "where are we going?"

It was 10:30 p.m., and Professor Handover was sitting quietly on his couch, sipping a Scotch, neat, just as he liked it, running various thoughts through his mind. They were coming up to class number eight, and then they would have twelve more to go to complete the twenty they had signed up for. Not a lot of time when you think about it. He needed to get a structure for the rest of the lessons. He knew where he was heading, and what the end result should be. This was his job. So he began making a list of subjects to cover, eight to twenty. Serious stuff this, and he wanted to get it right. He wanted to give these students, who he felt very close to, the right tools so they could go out into the world and live full, honest and satisfying lives. He had an obligation, and he would see it through. Their psychological well-being was his responsibility, at least until they left, anyway. Then it was down to the individuals and what they had taken away from the course.

Also, he needed to decide whether to pursue Lillie, knowing full well that it would start and it would finish. He was trying to decide if it would be worth the heartache that would follow, or if he could simply psychobabble the inevitable pain away. Well, it was worth a shot. He searched the records trying to find a phone number, his decision made.

Lillie's phone rang, and she had a gut instinct about who was on the other end. "Hello."

There was a cough. "Hello, Lillie, it's Professor Handover here, but since this is a private call, it's Friedrich. I was wondering if you would care to have dinner with me this weekend. Are you free?"

"Yes, I am, Professor…whoops, I mean, Friedrich. How about tomorrow, shall we say 8:00 p.m.? Just let me know the restaurant and address and I will meet you there."

She preferred to be under her own steam so she could go when and if it all became uncomfortable. On this point they were like minded.

They met at Angelino's, at the north end of town, close enough to walk. It was a quiet, rather romantic atmosphere inside, with that family feel that only Italian restaurants seem to be able to manage. He was in blue jeans, a white shirt and blue jacket, and she had thrown together one of her more alluring concoctions: multi coloured sheath dress, funky half biker boots and a string of beads round her neck. They both ordered pasta and red wine, and neither of them wanted a first course. The wine was served, and the conversation began. Both were aware that this dinner would either lead them to bed, or in the other direction. The outcome was by no means certain.

Exactly two and half hours later, they were in Friedrich's apartment making love.

That same evening…

Penelope and Max had decided to meet up again at the same bar where they had their first conversation. The flirtation was always visible between them, but they were both very cautious about letting it show. Drinks in hand, they found a quiet corner to sit and talk in.

"So Max, here we are again, back where we started but quite a few steps down the road, wouldn't you say? What do you think? Are we the same people?"

"Well, Pen, that's a loaded question because, on one side, I am a firm believer that you never really change your essence; no matter what happens, who you are is written in stone in your heart and soul. But you can add to who you are or subtract. So personally speaking, I have discovered some hidden issues, and, very surprisingly, I have found that I like vulnerability, at least in the opposite sex."

"I assume you are talking about Patricia. It's obvious to see you are very fond, and dare I say it, protective of her, as she is vulnerable with a capital V."

There was an awkward silence as they sipped their drinks. Max had to box clever with this one because, yes, he found Patricia attractive, but he also found Penelope attractive, irresistibly so actually: he was caught between a rock and a hard place. Finally, he decided on the unadulterated truth… why try and skirt around it, never works anyway, go straight to the point, yep.

"Okay, Pen, I am glad you posed the question, and I do owe you an honest answer. I owe me an honest answer too. I do find Patricia very appealing in a kind of puppy dog way. Her needs shine through and make a man feel very, dare I say it, masculine! I have not done anything about it because I am afraid that this is a momentary fascination, and if I started anything it will burn for a few hours and then she will die in the ashes… and that is just not fair. She has been hurt enough. But at the same time, she is now irresistible and I have not completely made up my mind yet as to whether to pursue it or not."

Penelope tried to keep any reaction to this under wraps, but it wasn't easy. It wasn't that she was in love with Max, but, and this is a big but, she definitely had feelings for him. She had to be very careful about what she said next.

"Well, Max, maybe you should take a leap of faith and stop trying to think it all through, trying to make something logical out of feelings which are anything but logical.

"I would say to you, especially knowing what I think I know about your psyche, you need to pursue this, you need to take a chance. Just the fact that you are having a battle within yourself to me says only one thing. That you are nervous about your feelings. And that, my friend, is exactly what this course should be teaching you. You cannot control where your heart falls. And, as you have already expressed, if it is only a momentary infatuation, so be it, just go and feel it."

Taking a pause to sip her drink, she decided to really bite the bullet.

"Let's cut to the chase, shall we? I don't think I am wrong in stating the obvious that you and I are attracted to each other, from day one. But now there is Patricia in the picture. I don't want to predict or presume, but my humble opinion is that you need to get this out of your system, and only then can we explore *our* future. Shame we haven't got a crystal ball, eh! Still, who really wants to know the future, not knowing is half the fun of getting there. Go on your love safari, happy hunting!"

They took a long beat looking into each other's eyes, understanding and accepting, for sure a match made in heaven.

"Cheers." They clinked glasses and walked back to their respective apartments quietly.

The same night, in Professor Handover's apartment…

They had thrown off their clothes and inhibitions following the bottle of red they consumed at dinner, leaving a trail of lust from the front door to the bed like so many breadcrumbs. And now that the deed was over, and both were slightly more sober, there was an awkward silence. Lillie lit a cigarette to bridge the gap, Friedrich sipped a little water from his glass on the side table. Lillie spoke first.

"Well, that was very nice, I must say. I did wonder if we would end up in bed or not, and here we are. What do you think? Was this a mistake? Are you okay? Are you sorry about what happened? Was it as you thought it would be? Hmm, I am babbling of course. A little unsure and a little embarrassed, to be honest. Your turn!"

Friedrich, being the elder by quite a few years, did not feel the need to cover the space with mindless chatter, but at the same time, he did need to respect Lillie's feelings and at least try to answer. He took another slow sip of water.

"Of course, it was nice, and possibly nicer than I expected. You must understand, at my age, there is always a long time between drinks. You are quite lovely dressed, and undressed, undressed being the operative word. Isn't it funny how having sex can bring out the vulnerability in someone? And I mean you. Not me. I am too long in the tooth for that. I do not regret this whatsoever, but I will point the question back at you. Do *you* think this was a mistake? Don't try and logic it out, just speak from your heart, your gut, your instinct, whatever you want to call it. Just say it without editing. How do you feel?"

Lillie dragged slowly on her cigarette, not in any hurry to answer. She smoked, she stretched, enjoying the afterglow of good sex, drawing the moment out if she dared.

"Mmm delicious… so, how do I feel? Do you mean besides being satisfied?" she said, trying her best to look innocent and failing miserably.

"No, I am not sorry it happened… not at all. I think it was inevitable. And I do hope for a repeat performance soon. But I would not be being truthful if I didn't say to you, I don't know how long this will continue for. We are different generations with different attitudes and needs, and, well, I just am not sure where this is going, or indeed where it can go. Also, it has just now occurred to me, how do we manage this in class? Surely the fact that we have slept together will become obvious to anyone with the slightest bit of ability to read body language. Over to you, Professor!"

"Good question, about the class. Yes, it is always apparent when two people have been intimate. There is a closeness in every gesture. There is a softer speaking voice, a lingering touch, a lingering look. Oh yes, it's obvious.

"I would not like to try and cover this up, but rather let it speak for itself. We are two grown up people and don't have to justify ourselves and I don't intend to. Class eight is coming up and for me it will be business as usual. And if any questions about our relationship do come up, well, for the sake of the course and what I am supposed to be teaching you, I believe we should be candid and open. And as for where this will go… that, my dear, is written in the stars."

Lillie looked at him, digesting what he had just said.

"Okay, Professor, message received loud and clear. You may have just fucked me, but don't you dare flunk me!"

They both laughed out loud, and then round two.

Penelope spent all day Sunday waiting in her room, thinking about the situation with Max, wondering what was or wasn't going to happen with Patricia, and how she would feel if it did happen. She knew she had feelings for him, and that the feelings were reciprocated, but she also knew this infatuation had to run its course if they were to have any chance at all. By the time evening came around, she had put it in a safe place in her mind, and slept like a baby, trusting that everything would happen just as it should.

Peter spent his Sunday in much the same way, thinking about his feelings for Lillie. He couldn't have stated it more clearly that he was indeed interested. He also knew without a shadow of a doubt that there was an attraction between her and the professor. He imagined them having the affair that he knew was on the cards. Could he still pursue her? Would he be eaten up with jealousy and resentment? Would his heart be broken? Would it be worth the trouble? Every instinct was screaming to him that this weekend the deed would be done. And she had agreed to see him next weekend. Well, class eight is tomorrow, he thought, I will have my answer about how I feel then. I will certainly be keeping a close eye on their body language.

Patricia spent her weekend looking through her old photo album. She did this whenever she had an issue that required her to step out of her comfort zone. This flirtation with Max was speeding up! And, as much as she wanted to throw caution to the wind, she hesitated. She had had too much heartache and was trying very hard to understand her weaknesses and go beyond them, hence her signing up for this course. She wanted to be able to apply logic to her life. She was determined. She did not expect to meet somebody like Max. Also, she was very aware that he and Penelope had a thing going on. She was also aware that they had not done anything about it yet, and that she, Patricia, was the reason for that. By the time Sunday evening rolled around she had decided that, if he asked, she would go out for a date with him and see where the road would lead them. Maybe she would ask him out. Now that would be one for the books. Shy, unassuming Patricia taking the first step. She finally fell asleep just after midnight with a smile on her face and the term 'passive aggressive' running round her brain.

Edmund spent his weekend quietly. There was something skipping around the edges of his mind that he could not quite grasp. All his life he had been invisible. No one got in, and no one got out. Why was that? Why was he so closed? Even taking into consideration his upbringing, it was no excuse. Even in this class he found it hard to open, only on a very surface level. He was beginning to feel like he had an emotional block, something from a long time ago that was buried in his psyche. Something he didn't dare remember. He had had these thoughts before and was always able to shove them on the emotional shelf out of the way. But not this time. He forced himself to dig deep, deeper than he ever had. He had no idea how long he had sat there thinking. Slowly, a hazy memory began to filter through. He sat calmly and waited for it to become clear, knowing he was on the brink of an important piece of the jigsaw puzzle that was Edmund.

Finally, the clouds parted, as he remembered in graphic detail being raped by one of his father's friends, at the age of eight. Oh my God.

Class 8

Penelope, Max, Patricia, Lillie, Peter and Edmund filed into the class and took what by now were their regular seats. There was an unnatural silence, which was probably down to nobody knowing what to expect next.

"Welcome back, everyone. There are twelve more meetings to go after today so I am tightening up the schedule so we can get through everything I need to teach you. The rest of the classes will be themed, except the very last one, which I have a little surprise planned for. So, today's topic will be how we face our demons and conquer them. We have covered a lot of ground already, and we have all shared very painful memories of growing up. In other words, the things we had to overcome to survive. But today's lesson will focus on a painful moment that was helpful to us, a moment that allowed us to see ourselves clearly, our weaknesses especially, and to face them bravely and march into adulthood. Last class I told you about the little boy going upstairs and getting his mother's suitcase so she could leave his dad. And, to start us all off, I will go first.

"This was an important moment in my development. Even though I hated the way my parents argued, my choice would never have been for them to separate. This is rarely any child's choice. I remember climbing those stairs. Every step took me closer to the dreaded suitcase and the inevitable flight of my beloved mother, which I inadvertently was helping her to do. The mother I adored and pitied in equal measure. I didn't really have a choice though. I had to do as I was asked.

"What this left me with is an acceptance of the things I cannot control. It is a valuable lesson and in my later years gave me a certain freedom from responsibility. And it gave me a tool with which to separate my mind from my heart. I have been doing this ever since, ninety-nine per cent of the time successfully. But, may I add, I am not pretending this is a good thing, and in fact in the end it may be more damaging to me as a functioning individual, well balanced, and... not alone. So, that's my character in a nutshell. I took it onboard and tried to turn it into a positive aspect of my personality.

"Who's next?"

Max decided he should go next, for no reason other than he should go next, so he did.

"This may be the time for me to reveal my deepest and darkest." Taking a huge deep breath, he continued. "There was this girl in junior high school. Very pretty, petite, and intelligent. A nice family from the more exclusive end of town. Not my normal type at all. I just wanted to walk down the other side for once. Anyway, I pursued her with my leather jacket, hair slicked back, the bad boy come to conquer, and conquer I did.

"We were an item for a while, maybe three months or so, when she fell pregnant, at fifteen. I was just sixteen. Well of course, I wanted nothing to do with this, and talked her into getting an abortion, much against her beliefs. I was the strong one though, and eventually got my way. So we aborted our child and then split up. She never forgave me. This was my wake-up call. I had, indirectly, taken a human life, and I have been haunted by it ever since. And, quite possibly, I destroyed the girl in the process. Women never get over this kind of thing, not truly. Even though I am honest enough to say I would probably make the same choice again. Sixteen is no age to become a dad. The shame of it sticks. From that moment on I changed inside. I killed the softness in me and became the man I am now. I had to let a lot of emotion go out with the bathwater. I had to close my heart to survive. What it has left me with is the following. I don't think I deserve to be a father. I forfeited my right. And I don't deserve to either love or be loved. I am an emotional shell, yet I still hope for somebody to come and crack me open.

"Phew. I don't have any idea why I decided to unload that piece of baggage at this moment, but I have. But, in my favour, I have accepted that I am stuck with me, so to speak; and that's okay."

He sat down.

This was one hell of a story, which firmly established lines of trust within the students. This one admission could open everyone to reveal their deepest darkest.

Professor Handover slowly rose from his chair and took centre stage so to speak.

"Very good, Max... very good indeed. I think it's time for a little Freud. His very basic psychosexual development can be used in this instance. First the oral stage from birth to one year. Next, the anal stage from one to three. Third, phallic stage, from three to six years; fourth, latent period, six to puberty, and finally genital stage from puberty to death. It seems to me, Max, that you are stuck in the latency phase. Your assignment, and indeed our assignment as a class together, is to find a way to push you into the genital stage, without any cockups." God, he thought, I am funny, why is no one laughing? "Does anyone have any comments to make, helpful or otherwise?"

Penelope stood up, almost too fast.

"Yes, Penelope. Go ahead."

"I for one love Freud. If I am translating this correctly, Professor, the latency period is taking stock and cooling off. I would say this is for sure where you are stuck, Max. Maybe you could try to travel back in time, to your id before it became your ego, or superego, find that space in you that felt the shame, owned the guilt, and at some point pushed it away where you couldn't see it anymore... if you could find that place, play the movie again, allow yourself to feel those feelings again, and then make a conscious effort to *not* push them away this time but live with them, then I think they would become part of the better you that you are striving to be. And, maybe, if you are brave enough, find that girl. A grown-up conversation is in order. This is unfinished business, the way I see it."

Penelope and Max had their moment, eyes locked in understanding of the soul. Watch this space!

"Thank you, Penelope, for that insight. Very professionally done. I'm impressed.

"Anyone else have something to share? We seem to be getting down and dirty today, which is fine with me," he said, looking directly at Lillie, a brief underlying meaning reflected in his eyes.

She stood up.

"Okay, in one of the classes I told you all that jealousy and resentment from other people was my trigger, and that I have always held onto my uniqueness to balance this out. Well, years ago, I found myself in a situation that made me behave badly. Here is what happened.

"I was again at a party with some friends, the booze and the conversation were flowing, and I must say, I was on particularly good form, witty, charming, and looking good. I held the floor. Everyone was enjoying my 'show'… including myself. Then, in walked this girl. My God, she was a beauty, but not in a classic way. In fact, if you dissected all her attributes they didn't fit together, yet somehow, they did. She studied the room as she entered, in charge, and full of confidence, and she stood there quietly. Charisma plus! Slowly the conversations dried up as one by one we all gravitated towards this stranger in the room. Introductions were made. She had us all charmed within fifteen seconds. I hung back and observed, realising I was reacting exactly how other girls had behaved towards me many times…. and I hated myself for it; yet I couldn't stop the feeling. Suddenly, I was not the centre of attention anymore, and I didn't like it one little bit. The jealousy was deep down and erupting into a fire. I had no idea I had this kind of resentment in me, since I was always the recipient of it before tonight. Then, I stumbled, and emptied my drink all over her. I apologised profusely of course, knowing inside that it was no accident. I wanted to mess her up, and I did. She handled it perfectly, didn't get flustered, asked for some paper towels, and dried herself off. At some point our eyes met and I saw in that instant that she knew what I had done, and that she knew why I had done it. I was exposed and I was humiliated. I made my excuses and left. This was a soul-searching moment for me and from that point on, I became non-judgemental, or tried to be non-judgemental, anyway. What choice did I have? It taught me one of life's big lessons. We all have these demons inside of us…. it just takes the right set of circumstances to set it off. And even though jealousy towards me can still affect me, I try not to let it control me

111

anymore, and I also try and forgive whoever is doing it. Most importantly, I accept my failings… I am only human. We are all only human, after all."

Everyone took a good long look at Lillie, reassessing their previous opinions of her character. She was always exotic, interesting but closed, and now, a new string to her bow, so to speak, vulnerable too. Very unusual combination, and very appealing. Both Professor Handover and Peter had basically the same thought: she is a complicated soul and would be fascinating to figure out. The professor of course had a head start.

"So, Lillie, you discovered a piece of yourself that you didn't like, and you tried to turn a negative into a positive with your determination to change that trait. Sometimes, these traits cannot be changed, but the realisation of it, and attempting to do something about it, is better than staying asleep to your foibles. Well done you.

"Peter, let's hear what you have to say on this subject."

"As I have already spoken about - indeed, we all have - I came from a non-communicative family. I accepted this but was not happy about it.

"I remember being unexpectedly alone with my father in the kitchen one afternoon. He had taken the day off work because he wasn't feeling too good, and I was just home from school, and we started to talk, and I mean really talk. It had never happened before, and it never happened again. I started asking him questions, what kind of parents he had (they had died before I was born), and their relationship. I asked him if they were close, if they 'talked'… I was on a roll and couldn't stop. He seemed to be surprised at my interest in his childhood, but nevertheless started to open up. He told me about his two sisters and how one of them, my Aunty Jane, had shamed the family by getting pregnant at fifteen years old, how his brother, my Uncle Wayne, was put in a home for disturbed children for five years, and how his other sister, my Aunty Mary, was a jealous, nasty, vindictive bitch who was unkind to everyone. His mother, my Grandma Pendergast, was, he said, a very bitter, unfulfilled woman who did nothing but have children, cook meals, do the laundry and perform her wifely duties whenever requested, and his father, my Grandpa Pendergast, took the strap to him for the slightest infraction. I saw the movie of his life play across his eyes with such pain. I was sorry I had asked these questions. These were memories that were probably best left buried. We parted that afternoon with a silent understanding. On his part he tried to explain why he was, indeed, non-communicative, and on my part, some kind of understanding and acceptance. This was something I had to think about very carefully in private. And I did. It was around that time that I discovered the subterfuge of humour. Laughing can cover a multitude of sins. This conversation changed my approach to life, changed my character, and brought out my natural talent for comedy. It enabled me to roll along a lot easier by burying the underlying issues. But if I am being honest, the price was very high, yes indeed, very high."

Professor Handover took charge.

"Okay class, these three stories have taken up a lot of time today, but maybe that's a good thing. They were in depth and interesting and deserve to be thought about. We will continue where we have left off today in class number nine. And at that class I will give you the basic outlines for the remaining eleven sessions. Thank you, and see you next time."

He brushed against Lillie and motioned her to hang behind. They needed to talk. She busied herself faffing around to delay her departure and tried not to make it obvious. Luckily the rest were talking amongst themselves and didn't seem to notice, except for Peter, who noticed everything. Yep, as he suspected, the deed had indeed been done.

The professor sat down in the vacant seat next to Lillie's. He wasn't sure what he was going to say but thought it better that he didn't take time to consider it. So he just blurted out whatever came to mind, which was very unlike him, being a psychology teacher. He should have been able to take a step back, pause, and then speak, but he didn't. He stroked her arm tentatively, not sure it if would be appreciated or not in public so to speak, and let his thoughts and feelings roll out.

"So, my exotic, delectable and now surprisingly vulnerable Lillie, how do you feel about things, about us? Are you comfortable with the situation? Do you want it to continue? And before you ask, I do want it to continue, at least until it's over." He chuckled.

"Well, now that you mention it, I must admit I am a little unsettled for various reasons. Yes, of course, it was very pleasurable and yes, I would like to keep it going.

"But where is it going? That's the big question. First, there is the age difference, and you are my professor, and how Freudian is that! Are we both getting too involved with a romance that is bound to end? And my instincts tell me it will end. Will it be worth the pain? I mean, I am younger and will recover, but you, I just don't know. I don't want to be the cause of your heartache, in fact I have never wanted to be the cause of anyone's heartache, and that has been my problem my whole life. You may be betting on the wrong horse. And of course, Peter is waiting on the sidelines for this to fizzle out, as I am sure you know already, being the intuitive person you are. How do *you* feel?"

"How do I feel? Usually with my hands." Another chuckle; God, I'm funny, he thought to himself. "I have asked these questions prematurely. I know that. But I feel the need to clarify. In all honesty, and I do want to level with you, I could fall for you in a big way, and before I allow myself to fall, I need to know what *we* are, or even if we are a 'we'. Your thoughts were truthful and appreciated. Even with these warnings as such, I would still like to have a few more encounters, and then reconsider how we both feel, if that's okay with you of course. I don't want to force you, but I don't feel we have given 'us 'a chance to be anything yet other than a one-night stand. And yes, I do know Peter has a serious crush on you, you would have to be blind, deaf and dumb to not see that every time he looks at you. It doesn't bother me, it's a free country, and none of can choose in matters of the heart. So what do you think? Would you like to have dinner on Saturday, then back to my apartment for some soft music and love making?"

Throwing caution to the wind, Lillie softly replied, "Okay," thinking to herself, what the hell, let's ride the ride and see where it takes me. My boundaries have been established and I have nothing to lose except my time.

Fixing his best seductive stare into her eyes, the professor replied, "Okay, that's a date," thinking to himself, what the hell,

114

it's been a long time since I've ridden this ride, let's see where it takes me. She has made her expectations clear, now let's see what I can do about moving the goal posts.

And so, the games began, from the two different perspectives!

On Friday evening the professor spent many hours working out the topics of discussion for the remaining classes. Not many weeks left. Not a long time to establish things with Lillie. Oh well, it will do what it does, he pondered quietly to himself, just got to roll with it. The main thing I must do is make the plans for the remaining classes. I think we can dissect Freud's stages of psychosexual development, that would be good. Class nine, we'll cover the oral stage from birth to one year, class ten, anal stage, from one to three, class eleven, phallic stage from three to six, class twelve, latency period, six to puberty, and class thirteen, the genital stage from puberty to death, then just seven more classes to go. Lets see, class fourteen we can discuss id, ego and superego, then classes fifteen to eighteen, the basic personality types, openness, conscientious, extroversion, agreeableness, and neuroticism. This last one should be interesting. And finally, class nineteen, where I spring my little surprise on them, and twenty, we party. Okay, this looks good to me, and workable. He settled down for the night to do some notes. Lots to do, lots to do, lots to do, he thought, nudging his Saturday date into the rear area of his mind.

Max lay on his bed completely clothed, arms underneath his head, thinking. Should I or shouldn't I? I know she will be receptive. Question is, do I want to go there? He considered Penelope. We have a thing going on between us, but I am sure it will still be going on between us even if I do see Patricia. It's an itch I must scratch and until I scratch it, Pen and I will go nowhere, which would be a damn shame. He dialled Patricia's number and made a date for Saturday evening, drinks and dinner. She didn't hesitate to say yes, not for a millisecond. As if she was expecting the phone call! Done and dusted. Let the good times roll.

Things were taking interesting turns amongst the six psychology students, not to mention the professor too. Where was the road leading to?

Saturday morning arrived. Max decided to get a haircut on the spur of the moment. Then he would shower and shave and put on his tightest jeans, favourite t-shirt and jacket for his upcoming encounter with the fragile Patricia. I wonder what she looks like naked? he thought, smirking in the mirror.

Patricia awoke with a splash of excitement, diluted with a little apprehension. What will I wear, what will we talk about, what am I doing? She lazed around, trying her best to relax, and finally it was time to start getting ready. Ready for what, she thought to herself, choosing a virginal white ruffly dress with a nice pair of shoes.

Lillie slept in quite late, finally surfacing around 11:00 a.m. She had lain awake the night before pondering her decision to keep seeing the professor. She wasn't sure if it was a cruel thing to be doing, because she was absolutely one hundred per cent convinced it could not go anywhere other than a few meetings: or would it be crueller to not even give him a chance to prove himself? Prove himself as to what and to whom? "Boy oh boy, I am setting myself a high perch from which to fall. Hope it's not me who does the falling. Karma can be a bitch," she said to the four walls.

At 6:30, she had a nice hot bubble bath, put a little make up on and went to the closet to pick out her dinner date outfit.

Professor Handover was feeling pretty good, having made his plan for the rest of the course. He was happy with it and could now relax and look forward to his dinner date with the delectable, exotic Lillie. He put a bottle of Bollinger in the refrigerator and two nice champagne glasses to chill in preparation for where he was certain their dinner date would end up, in his bed. He was quietly confident.

Max was already seated at the bistro when Patricia arrived, nursing a G & T.

He stood up and gave her a light hug and a chaste kiss on the cheek; he didn't want to move in too quickly and scare her away. He pulled out her chair, like the perfect gentleman he wished he was.

"You look very nice tonight, Patricia. What would you like to drink?"

"I will have whatever you're having. You look good yourself, Max."

Max signalled the waiter, motioning one more please, which arrived quickly, along with the small menu.

Not wanting to waste time reading the damn thing Max blurted out, "What can you recommend?"

"Well sir, we have a special tonight of coq au vin, served with steamed broccoli and spinach, and new potatoes on the side."

"Patricia, is that okay for you?"

"Yep, sounds perfect."

"And a large mineral, and a nice bottle of Chardonnay."

There was an embarrassed pause once the waiter had left, then they both started to talk at once, which broke the ice.

Max and Patricia enjoyed their evening between the sheets. Her vulnerability took a back seat in bed, much to Max's surprise. Quite a wildcat!

The professor and Lillie went for the second round, which was every bit as good as the first.

Their lost weekends were over. Back to reality.

Class 9

Everyone filed in right on time. Two of the students had a distinct blush on their cheeks, noticed by Penelope and of course Peter, and accepted by Penelope and Peter.

"Welcome, everyone. Let's continue where we left off. There are three more to go, Patricia, Penelope and Edmund. Patricia, you're looking quietly confident today, how about you start us off?"

"So, as you all know by now, I am a sad sack, I gather unhappiness without even trying, have very little self-confidence, and always get my heart broken, which leaves me feeling not good enough; not a nice feeling to get you through life. You would think that would make me a compassionate person, ready to help those in need, those with similar deficiencies as myself. Normally this is the case, but there was this one time..."

Long pause as she fidgeted, tapped her fingers, and played with her hair.

"There was this girl at school, Linda Scherer. She wasn't bad looking, blonde, medium height. Her family were well off. But she had learning difficulties. One day the teacher asked me to stay after class, which I did. She said Linda was having problems settling in. She was awkward and shy, and people did poke fun at her. Would it be possible for me to take her on board and help her out? She thought I was the right person to do this. So I said, sure.

"I began the next day, hanging with her at lunch time, riding next to her on the bus home, trying to bring her out of her shell. This went on for a few weeks, and I began to feel a certain strength, that *I* was not the weak one, the sad one, the needy one: she was. And I was in charge! I felt powerful for the first time in my life. Slowly but surely my attitude started to change. I had control here. I am ashamed to say, I started to be unkind, making jokes at her expense. My rock bottom came when I threw her gym shoes out the bus window. This got a huge laugh from everyone. I felt terrible.

"I went home and cried myself to sleep. How could I of all people do something like that? It was my wakeup call because I made a vow to never step out of character again. And I have kept that vow. I apologised the next day to Linda and remained her friend until her untimely death in an automobile accident when she was fifteen. I still visit the grave regularly, and even had a cast iron pair of gym shoes made to lay upon the grave. In a way, Linda was responsible for giving me the strength to be exactly who I am. And for that I am eternally grateful."

"Thank you, Patricia. That's a sad story indeed and very revealing. Okay, Penelope. Off you go."

"Mine is short and sweet, just like me." She giggled. "I fell in love with a married man when I was seventeen and had a yearlong affair. This went against everything my Catholic upbringing had taught me. It amazed me that I had no guilt whatsoever, and that I could even picture him with his wife, and it didn't bother me. I just wanted what I wanted and was young enough to go out and get it. When it eventually ended, my call, it left me thoroughly ashamed of myself. How could I do that to another women? They had two kids as well. Disgusting. So, I also made a vow. Never to be the other woman again. Never to do to anyone else what I would not want done to me. Not in this lifetime. And I haven't and I won't. When I do fall again, hopefully with the one this time, it will be forever. The whole episode was a point of no return for me. I found my true moral code. And can I add, I don't fall in love easily either, but when I do, I will go the distance. Especially after seeing the heartbreak my sister's divorce caused, when I do finally marry, that's it. I will stay married. Strange how an illicit affair can end up defining not only who you are, but who you are not. Don't know which is more important."

"Thank you, Penelope. And now, for the final speaker, Edmund, you're up."

"Well, I guess you could say I have been the most unforthcoming student in the class, except when I floored Max!

That was the only time in my life I have ever been so provoked, and I thank you again for hitting the nail on the head.

"I went back and forth wondering whether to share what I have to say, because it is highly personal; but hell, if I don't put it on the table now, I never will.

"I was sitting in my room last weekend and found my mind was wandering around, remembering all sorts of forgotten instances that I had successfully shelved. I was having a quiet glass of wine, which probably loosened my thought process. Suddenly, I started to feel like there was an obstruction in my brain. Usually, and this has happened before, I try to stop the fog from lifting. But this time I allowed myself to go with it.

"I was raped by one of my dad's friends. I must have only been about eight years old. I can now remember it in detail, and it is not pleasant, and I do not wish to share the details. Suffice to say, it was a key incident in my development, causing me to close in on myself. Wow, and to remember it now! What a shock to the system! I am determined to get this out, to examine it, dissect it, go deep inside and feel it, and then, hopefully, put it where it belongs."

The class was silent for a good five minutes. Nobody knew quite what to say. Edmund had been almost too revealing. But the flip side was, everyone could sympathise and understand him a little better. Peter seemed quite affected by his story and stared long and hard at Edmund for a good five minutes.

"Thank you everyone for your candour, your honesty, and your bravery. Onwards and upwards we go.

"I want to touch today on Freud's oral stage. I am paraphrasing here: this is where we all have gratification through the mouth through rooting and stimulation... pure pleasure, which mentally never leaves us, it just changes form. And if we don't wean ourselves from this at the correct time we become orally fixated; this can result in drinking, eating and smoking disorders, and nail biting. Interesting. Can I ask who of you was breast fed? Hands up."

Five raised their hands, excluding Penelope.

"Okay, Penelope, since you are the only non-breast fed one here, just for argument's sake, how do you relate to that? Obviously, you still derived oral pleasure from the bottle."

"Yes, Professor, I do have an opinion on that. Maybe because I never had this mouth to breast connection with my mother, this pleasure has always remained firmly in my personal erogenous zone, nothing to do with nourishment, and in fact I doubt, when and if I have a child, I will want to breast feed. So I never had to wean myself off anything."

Max piped up, "Well, I was breast fed and do have a slight problem with drinking, not bad, but it's there, if I don't watch it."

Patricia added, "And here I am a self-confessed nail biter."

Peter said, "Yep, me too, down to the quick sometimes."

Edmund added, "None of those apply, so obviously I didn't get fixated, probably shelved it."

Lillie said last, "And me, I smoke."

"So, class, whether your adult problems are a result of fixation in the oral stage of development, no one can say, but it is interesting to note the results. In fact, you could say, these results 'suck'." He chuckled at his own joke.

"We're done and dusted for the day. In class ten we will try and get through both the anal and the phallic stage. Very good, everyone, very good indeed. We are getting down to the nitty gritty of this course now, so make sure you are prepared. I will leave with you a quote from Baron in 1998, psychology can be defined as 'the science of behaviour and cognitive processes, any observable actions by an organism, on thoughts, mental images, and how one reasons, one's memories' and so on. See you next time."

Everyone gathered their books and filed quietly out of the room. They were all busy thinking.

Class 10

It was a rainy day outside as the usual suspects filed into the room and sat down in their usual chairs.

"Welcome, everyone. We have nine lessons left after today and lots to cover, so let's not waste a minute. Right, today we are doing first the anal and then the phallic stage of psychological development. They are connected very closely. Freud teaches that the anal stage is learning to control your bodily functions, thereby leaving us with a sense of accomplishment and independence. There are two sides to this which involve the parent or parents, and how they teach said child. I personally believe this is the first time we have a direct result according to the method of our parenting. Make or break if you like, to pee or not to pee." God I am funny, he thought, I wonder why no one ever laughs.

"Too lenient, and the child can develop an expulsive personality, and become messy, wasteful and destructive when they become adults; too strict, or too early, they can develop an anal-retentive personality and become stringent and obsessive.

"So, for argument's sake, let's examine the outcomes for a moment, and then, with a show of hands, how many of you feel you were trained too leniently?"

Peter, Penelope, Patricia and Edmund all raised their hands.

"Would any of you like to clarify your answer?"

They all looked at each other, seemingly a little reluctant to speak out. This was embarrassing stuff.

Peter stood up and bit the bullet.

"Okay. Since I come from a non-communicative family anyway, I would say my parents, mainly mom as it was her duty being a housewife, was too lenient. I can't remember her punishing me for wetting the bed, which I believe I did quite frequently. Or forcing me to sit on one of the potties. I do however remember watching my older brother sit there. Perhaps she thought I would learn by example. And I did.

"I remember finally trying it out all alone, sitting in the kitchen. No-one was there to praise me, or indeed wipe me when I was done. I did my first number two! Then I simply stood up and walked away. Now, looking at myself as an adult, I am messy, I can be wasteful if I don't watch myself, and I have had my moments of destruction."

Penelope was next.

"I can relate to your story, Peter, and confirm it. When you have older brothers and sisters, there is far less pressure for training to be a problem. I remember my mom telling me that she could remember every detail of my two eldest siblings, illnesses, worries, teaching, training, all adding to sleepless nights over whether you were doing it correctly or not. By the time number three comes along, you don't worry about it, and the kids kind of raise themselves with the help of the other kids. So, lenient for sure.

"And me, as an adult, I can say that I can be expulsive given the right circumstances and can be messy. I did have a tendency to be destructive but recognised that in my teens and reined it in. And that's my toilet story. I wonder at what age toilet humour comes into play? Just a thought. Okay… I'm wiped out."

Patricia took the floor.

"I don't have a lot of memory of this stage either way, so I am assuming it leaned towards too lenient rather than too strict as the latter would have caused a negative reaction. Or possibly it was balanced. Anyway, I put my hand up because I thought it was the right response given the two choices. Saying that though, I don't have any of the characteristics described."

Edmund was next.

"My memory of this stage is that my mother was the kind who believed in letting nature take its course, and that once I got tired of that cold, damp feeling between my legs, I would want to learn how to control my bowels. So I was kind of left to fend for myself. And, since I had no siblings to imitate, I had to make it up as I went along.

"As an adult, I too can be very messy, and if, and I say if, I allowed myself, I could be destructive. Like Penelope, I rein that part in."

"Okay, Max and Lillie, could you share with us your opinions on this subject please."

Max went first.

"Well, in my case, it was way too strict from both sides as far as I can recall, although the memory is quite faded. My mom overdid it a bit. I had a problem with bedwetting for quite a few years, caused by my parents 'relationship I am sure, and I can still picture her pulling me out of the wet sheets and changing them begrudgingly no matter what the time was. She was not a happy person. And, my father, he just smacked my ass for everything. So, yes, too strict on both sides. And yes, I am anal retentive, although I think that's a polite word for it, and I am obsessive about almost everything I can think of."

Lillie stood up.

"So, I had very free-thinking parents, and you would have thought they would have been easy with all this stuff, but for some reason, they went the opposite way. Looking back on it with hindsight, I think they balanced out the easygoing way they lived their lives therefore they came down heavy on this. I remember learning to use the potty as being a very serious thing, very serious indeed. And as an adult I am stringent, I am mildly obsessive (is that allowed?) and anal retentive."

"Thank you, everyone. And now for the next development, which is the phallic stage from three to six years old. Many believe that this is where our real memory starts, but I beg to differ. I have flashes of things much younger than that, and as you have all shared, we all do. So, this is the phase when girls and boys start to realise the difference between them. The boys start to look at their dads as rivals for their mothers 'affections, called the Oedipus complex, wanting to possess them and replace the father, and at the same time fear punishment for feeling this way, which is known as castration anxiety… ouch! Very complicated. Very Freudian."

He paused for laughter which did not appear.

"And for girls it's the same system but the opposite way round, known as the Elektra complex. Freud says it's penis envy that never goes away. But not all psychologists agree with him. In fact, Karen Horney, interesting name in this context, says this is demeaning to women and that it is indeed the men that never get over the fact that they can't have children. Womb envy? Let's throw that open for discussion.

"Let's examine what Freud believes and what Miss Horney believes, and maybe we will find that, as is often the case with the truth, it's in the middle. Okay girls, do any of you feel like you suffer from penis envy? Think about it seriously, it's a hard question, and I don't want you to go off half-cocked." Goddamn, I'm so funny, he thought, as a small titter went round the room.

Lillie raised her hand.

"Well, if I am being perfectly honest, I do have a little of this. It manifests itself when I am angry and wish I was a man so I could knock somebody's block off, you know what I mean? One good punch, the answer to everything. God how I would love to do that sometimes, mid confrontation, splat, down they go... argument over."

Penelope raised her hand.

"Okay, if I have any penis envy at all, it is only ever in one circumstance, that's when I need to go to the toilet and there is a huge line to get in, while the man simply strolls in, unzips, does his business, shakes it off, and leaves. I think the big man upstairs has a lot to answer for designing our equipment the way he did."

The class chuckled.

Patricia put her hand up.

"Nope, not me. I am too vulnerable to even consider this question as viable, but I must admit, I did have a crush on my dad at this age, that I can remember vividly."

"Okay… and now let's go to the other side of the equation according to Miss Horney: do any of you gentleman suffer from womb envy?"

Peter stood up.

"I don't know if it's envy as such, but I do have a healthy respect for women and their ability to reproduce. It absolutely amazes me and is also just a little scary, but I think that's a normal and healthy attitude. Saying that though, I have never felt the need to reproduce. Children are not in my game plan. And as far as having feelings towards my mother, nope... zero. Too non-communicative a situation to develop anyway. Emotionally my family was a closed book."

Edmund was next.

"I do have womb envy. I am so jealous sometimes that the female species can become pregnant, grow a new human being in their wombs, and then produce a baby at the end of nine months. In fact, I would go as far to say, sometimes I wish I was a woman so I could experience this. I am in awe, totally. Maybe someday men will be able to make babies… well, I can dream, can't I? And to answer the Freud issue, I didn't have any complex feelings for my mother either."

And finally, Max.

"Womb envy, nope, not at all. The macho in me is quite happy to separate and respect both sexes. I am happy being a man, and happy women are women. No problem there. And, as far as my mother goes, nope, no hidden crushes there, too clouded by pity and the situation with my father that she allowed herself to live with. Which I guess had the added effect of not having penis envy either. If that's what a penis, i.e. my dad, meant, who the hell needs it. Maybe I am anti-penis."

Max sat.

"And that is a nice point to end class ten. Next time we will be moving onto the latency period from six to puberty, and now folks, it starts to get interesting. Class dismissed."

The group were animated on leaving this class. It was getting very interesting indeed. This is what they had signed up for. They naturally grouped together and began talking. Max, Penelope and Patricia walked one way, deep in conversation, and Peter and Edmund went the other way, also in deep conversation, leaving Lillie lagging behind, deep in thought.

"So, girls, what do you say we go for a pizza? My treat."

"Fine with me," said Patricia, managing to seem happy that Penelope was being asked too; after all, she and Max had slept together. And off they went to town.

Penelope, aware of everything, decided to tag along even though she was the gooseberry. This should be fun, she thought. She wanted to keep her hand in with Max.

126

Edmund suggested to Peter that they stop at a bar and get a drink, and that's what they did. "Strange thing to do," Edmund thought to himself.

Lillie went to her apartment and called the professor, inviting him to dine with her at 'their 'restaurant. He accepted.

Peter and Edmund stopped at Chequers, a nice quiet little bar just off campus, ordered a beer each, and chose a quiet table near the back. Peter had an agenda and jumped right in. His curiosity had been tweaked.

"Edmund, I must say I found your story both poignant and interesting. Do you mind, now that there are no other ears to hear you, sharing with me the details of your rape. It must have been horrific for you to have successfully blocked it for so long. I may be wrong, but I sense that you would love to share it with somebody, and indeed need to share it with somebody, so it may as well be me. How about it?"

They both sipped their beers through the pregnant pause in the conversation, and finally Edmund began to talk.

"Okay, Peter. I guess it's time to purge… I guess I am ready to purge. So, here we go.

"Funny that after blocking it for so long, as you rightly pointed out, it is crystal clear now, every detail as if it happened just yesterday. He was my dad's friend from work, nice looking, tall, intelligent and articulate, and very kind. In fact, he was everything I wished my dad was. And, most importantly, he always had time for me. He would ask the right questions, and really listen. I liked him a lot. He would always come into my room and spend about half an hour with me when he visited, explaining to mom and dad that we both connected and since he had no kids of his own, he enjoyed the experience very much. They accepted this for some reason, and so the grooming began. Looking back on it now, it *was* grooming. Each time we spoke he got a little closer, eventually abandoning the chair for the edge of the bed. We talked and talked and talked. I felt so appreciated. I felt heard for the first time in my life. It was a heady feeling. These bedroom sessions went on for about three months. Finally, as fate dictated, he arrived for his usual visit with my father, but they were out for the evening. And, looking back on it, I am sure he knew this, and indeed planned it all out. He asked if we could still have our usual half hour in my room. I saw no reason to say no, so in we went. This time though, there was no sitting on the edge of the bed, and softly talking; oh no, this time he said in a voice I did not recognise, "Take your clothes off now." I remember being totally confused at this new scenario, thinking perhaps it was a joke; I was too scared to not do as he asked. His face and manner were completely different. I got undressed and just stood there, shaking like a leaf. Somewhere deep inside, I knew what was going to happen, and I knew I should scream and run for my life, but I also knew I wanted it to happen in a strange kind of way. And I was curious. But my God, I was so young, so damn young. Anyway, he touched my privates, first making me get an erection, and of course that felt nice. He then touched himself until he was flying a full mast, he then pushed me onto the bed, turned me on my stomach, and thrust himself into my tiny little rectum. And it hurt, good God, did it hurt. It was all over in about three minutes.

"I was bleeding, he was satisfied. He got up, wiped himself off, put on his clothes and left the house. We never saw him again. I was left confused, humiliated and sore. I lost the soreness but have remained confused and humiliated my entire life. The story is out now, and I will never try to hide it again. So there you have it, Peter, the gory details. This horrific movie will play in my mind forever. And I am pretty sure I am actually gay. Yep, there I have said it… I think I am gay, and I am prepared to act on this revelation. In a way it's a relief to be out of a closet I didn't even know I was in!"

Peter stared at Edmund, and Edmund stared at Peter. They looked deep into each other's eyes, right down to the soul. For Peter, this feeling he was feeling was something he had suspected in himself for a long time, but being from a non-communicative family had made it easy to push it way down and concentrate on the opposite sex for his gratification. But subconsciously he always knew he had this in him. Edmund inched slowly forward, taking the lead. And then they kissed. It was an unexpected moment, but not an unwelcome one. One kiss, that's all it took. No words were spoken, they broke apart, finished their beers, paid the bill and walked quietly and quickly back to Peter's apartment, and did what came naturally. They were a couple from this evening on. This was a first for both. Strange how it all felt so natural.

Lillie and Professor Handover were eating a nice meal accompanied by a glass of red wine. They were getting comfortable with each other now. The boundaries had been drawn and they both respected them. Dessert came, followed by coffee.

"Friedrich, I want to ask you something. You know in class when Edmund told us that he had been raped as a child, do you think he may have sexuality issues? I mean to me he is kind of asexual, neither here nor there, but my instincts tell me he may be gay. And if so, as a psychology professor, do you think remembering this now may enable him to act upon his sexuality if indeed he is gay?"

"Hmm, this could happen. I must say, my instincts say the same thing and have done from day one. He is always uncomfortable in class in just about every situation. I hope this does bring him out. He needs to get in touch with himself.

"And, in fact, I will go one step further. It's about Peter. I have been observing him try and flirt with you since this course began. He knows about us of course and is waiting for his chance to step in and sweep you off your feet. But I must say, he lacks commitment, and he is not convincing. It's almost like he is going through the motions and acting out this flirtation. I wouldn't be at all surprised if he turned out to be gay too. And while we are gossiping... what about Max and Patricia? I'm pretty sure they have been to bed with each other. I don't think it will last at all because Max is just too masculine and self-centred for her and will end up hurting her, unless she is able to turn him around and make him more compassionate. The jury is still out on that. And of course, you must realise that Penelope has a crush on Max. And in my book, these two would be perfect together. Still, all is fair in love and war."

They finished their coffee deep in thought, and then went back to his apartment.

Max, Patricia and Penelope were sharing a large pizza with everything on it, washed down with a nice bottle of Chianti. Perfect combination.

"Good that you could join us, Penelope," said Patricia, managing to establish that 'us 'was Max and her, and they did indeed have a relationship. That's if you can call one night together a relationship!

"Yes, I am glad too. It's nice to hang out isn't it? So, tell me, how long has 'this 'been going on. Hope I am not being rude, but it is obvious to see."

Max looked very uncomfortable. He was not at all sure where this was going with Patricia but was smart enough to know that she was the kind that would fall quickly and heavily, and he was not sure if that was what he wanted… and he was attracted to Penelope, mind and body. What a quandary.

"We are at the beginning stages, Pen. The getting to know each other part. One night together does not a relationship make," said Max, rather unchivalrously.

Patricia was surprised and embarrassed at this response and excused herself to go to the ladies' room.

"I'm sorry," Pen jumped in immediately when Patricia was out of earshot, "I didn't mean to put you in that position. Guess I was curious at how it was going. It looks like you're in for a rough ride already, emotionally. My humble… she is too soft for you. Go gently there, and, let me take my one chance to say it… I am here when you're ready."

They looked at each other, a long look that spoke volumes. Battle lines had been drawn. They both knew it. When the fling was over, Pen and Max would get it together.

And Patricia would be hurt, very hurt. This was a given.

Patricia returned to the table, a little red eyed, and valiantly tried to put on a happy face with a positive spin on it… she failed miserably. They finished eating, divided the bill by three, and went outside, ready to say goodbye. Now the moment of truth. Would Max go his own way or accompany Patricia home? He looked at Pen with a 'trapped 'expression on his face, turned and looked at the needy Patricia, and guilt won. He took her arm and steered her in the direction of his digs. They said their goodnights, all three lonely in their own way.

Class 11

Everyone was seated and Professor Handover took the floor, anxious to get today's agenda started.

"So, boys and girls, we are doing the latency period today, and that's what you all are according to this stage of development… it covers six to puberty, when you are all indeed boys and girls. This is the period when your sexual feelings are inactive and repressed. You have other interests: school, hobbies, and peer relationships. Sexual urges are at the bottom of the list. It is an important stage when we develop our social and communication skills. Some get stuck in this stage, meaning they never grow up, which can lead to the inability to form mature relationships with anyone as an adult, or indeed fulfilling ones. Who would like to open the discussion on this subject?"

Patricia raised her hand.

"I just had a real response to this, an unexpected response, deep down, and I would like to explore it. It was when you said, 'be unable to form a mature relationship as an adult.' This is me. A hundred per cent. I know it and have always known it, but until this class and indeed this lesson, I could never locate or name it. I feel like a lightbulb has gone on in my mind. If I dig into my memory, I can remember this period, I was so involved in school, even had a crush on the popular girl at school, had lots of hobbies, and was quite comfortable in myself. If I could have, I would have stayed in this time frame. I was happy. I did not welcome puberty whatsoever. It scared the hell out of me. I believe I am stuck in the latency period. Question is, what the hell do I do about it?"

"Okay, boys and girls, this is an interesting way to tackle this. Does anyone have any suggestions for Patricia as to how she overcomes this, or does anyone think that it's fine and she should simply remain true to herself?"

Penelope took the floor. Speaking to the whole class, she began.

"What I am hearing from Patricia is that when puberty arrived, she was immediately afraid of being hurt. We have already heard about her childhood experiences, and indeed she was and has been hurt, and sorry to say, will probably continue to be hurt.

"I don't know if there is a way out of this or not. I am a believer that we are wired how we are wired." She turned directly to Patricia as she continued. "You must ask yourself if you are happy being the vulnerable soul you are, or do you want to shut off the soft side, and toughen up, which would help in the getting hurt stakes, but you would not be who you are anymore. It's a real melon scratcher. I would say, you accept you as you, you're soft and you pick the wrong guys time after time. I believe you have a choice though. Either change or accept yourself," she finished, with a sneaky glance at Max.

"Interesting take, Ms. Perfect, anyone else?"

Peter stood.

"Well, this period that we are discussing seems to me like the most important one. We are developing our id, ego and superego… sex is not getting in the way. We are making our way through the communicative vortex. We are creating our future personalities, with a few wrenches thrown in for good measure. Personally speaking, I can see exactly how I developed during this period. And like Patricia, I am finding this explanation of 'latency period 'very useful in explaining to myself why I am such a late bloomer. And I will leave it right there."

Max was next.

"Yes, I agree, we all must make our own decision whether to 'de-wire 'our natural tendencies. To me it's all about if it is hurting you or not. Nothing wrong with being vulnerable," he looked at Patricia pointedly, "but there must be a balance. Otherwise, every relationship you have will end up with you getting hurt, and your partner feeling guilty. It's a no-win situation. Both of you lose. Can I ask, have you ever been the cause of the pain in any relationship?"

Everyone's eyes were on Max and Patricia. They were eavesdropping on a personal conversation.

"Strictly speaking Max, in romantic relationships, the answer is no, I have never been the one to cause the hurt. But I don't believe any of us escape without getting our heart broken at least once, and maybe, just maybe, my day will come."

The professor walked around to the front of his desk and looked carefully at each of his pupils. After some thought, he began..

"Before we go any further today, I would like for us to come clean with each other about relationships that have developed between us since these classes began. I will go first, as I am sure it is obvious Lillie and I are in a relationship... of sorts."

Nobody looked in the slightest bit surprised.

"Okay," Max blurted out, "I have slept with Ms Vulnerable."

"And me," said Penelope, "I guess I am the virgin queen...well, a born-again virgin anyway."

This left Peter and Edmund to speak out. Lillie and the Professor exchanged a knowing look.

Peter stood up, glancing quickly at Edmund, trying to ascertain it if was okay. He looked like it was.

"So, I would say both Edmund and me were also stuck in this latency period. Yes, I have had girlfriends, but I can't say any of these relationships have been fulfilling, indeed I always felt like something was missing but could not put my finger on it.

"Then, the other night, quite unexpectedly..." He paused, quite flustered. "Edmund and I became a couple. There. I've said it. No more hiding, no more bullshit. We are both 'out'."

Edmund stood up, "I have nothing to add to that. It is what it is. And I for one am happy it's out."

There was a very long pause, as everyone processed this information.

"Well, well, well, students, if this isn't a turnout for the books! Busy little bees, each one of us. And there's poor Penelope all on her lonesome. This perfectly leads us into our final Freudian stage of psychological development, which is the genital stage, covering puberty to death. See you next time."

Lillie stayed behind to wait for the professor. Peter and Edmund walked out shoulder to shoulder, Max and Patricia held hands, and Penelope wandered off alone, looking thoughtful.

Class 12

Everyone filed in quietly and took their seats. They were all aware of the change in the atmosphere. Things had shifted. Relationships had been exposed. There was nowhere left to hide for any of them, including the professor.

"Good morning, class. So, off we go into the wild blue yonder, eh? Let me begin with some information concerning this final stage of development, which, if you are successful, results in settling down with a person in your twenties, give or take a few years. The sexual instinct now becomes a shared experience rather than self-pleasure, or it should do anyway. There are no hard rules." I am so funny, he thought. "If, however, you are denied the realisation of being in a successful relationship, sexual perversions may begin to appear. There are three main writers on neo analytical traditions worth looking at. Peter Blos, from 1979, whose theory of adolescent development emphasises the growth of autonomy from one's parents, and as he calls it, individuation. Harry Stack Sullivan, from 1953, says people need to develop a capacity for intimate relationships. But the one who resonates with me is Erik Erikson from 1968. He focuses on the quest for a sense of identity. In fact, as he puts it, identity vs. identity diffusion… which is a challenge to resolve your inner conflicts and get a true sense of who you are and where you are going. This sums it up for me. Finding our identity. And to quote I Ching, 'shake hands with ourselves'. Once we have done this, the rest of our lives will follow, ending of course in the inevitable ashes to ashes, dust to dust. 'Know thyself,' somebody very wise once said. Let's open the discussion on this subject. You are all in the genital stage and will remain in this until the final roll call, so… DO YOU KNOW WHO YOU ARE? Let's hear from Penelope first."

"I must admit, I have been analysing myself. I have been going deep inside and examining all the different relationships I have had with boyfriends, friends and family. I am like an onion that you must keep peeling, layer after layer. I am a dichotomy. I am strong as hell, yet thin skinned and hurt easily, I am independent yet vulnerable, I don't love easily but when I do, I fall hard. I feel like I am a compassionate person yet I can be cold to others' pain at times, considering it to be a weakness. I like people around and enjoy socialising but, if I am honest, I would like to have a magic wand so I could make them disappear when I've had enough. I would say I do not possess a middle ground. I am either up or down, happy or sad, the life of the party, or the party pooper, awake or asleep, extremely funny or extremely depressed. And the key word is, I like to be in complete control of my life. Summing up me, I would say I am comfortable in my skin and happy to continue down my road wherever it takes me. Bring it on, genital stage, I got this."

"Very well said, Ms Perfect. Who is next?"

"I'll have a go next," Peter said confidently.

"Okay, so if this is the stage of development for the rest of our lives, I guess I'd better be at peace with it. But I am wondering, do we not develop and change constantly? I mean to the end of our lives i.e. forever. Seems a long time. Even though I have come out late, I have indeed come out. It is now logical to me that my psyche will now go through many changes, how I look at the world, how the world looks at me, and who I am. Everything has changed. So, for me, this genital final stage of development has come quite late. Does it still work on the same theory or am I the cog in the wheel? Just throwing it out there."

Professor Handover answered.

"Peter, that's a good question and one worth debating. I have studied Freud my entire career and am very familiar with his stages of development and what they entail. I do believe this could be open for interpretation. I think, whether you stay on the same trajectory or change direction, I believe it means you are still on your true path, and the change is a part of it. Anyone else have an opinion on this?"

Max jumped in.

"I am not sure if that is the case. Surely if you have denied your true nature well into your adult life, this would change everything and would lead to a different kind of existence. Outcome and probability. Surely this must come into the equation, otherwise we are just robots following a map of sorts from birth to death. I would like to think we have some choice in the matter, otherwise why bother with any of it?"

Patricia added her two cents' worth.

"I think the answer is not black and white. I believe we do have a course to follow, but within that course there are opportunities to take the high road, the low road or the one in the middle. Each one reflects how you live your life, but it doesn't change the end of the story. So, yes, you have a choice, but it does lead to the same grave with a tombstone. But even with that grim reality in front of us, I believe we owe it to ourselves to live our lives as honestly as possible, along with whatever obstacles appear."

The professor looked proudly at his students; they were coming along very nicely indeed.

Lillie took the floor.

"It looks like the big word here is 'choice'. When you think about it, we are faced with choices every single day. I don't think though that the choices we make, good or bad, have anything to do with our actual path. It's just diversions in between life and death. I don't think there are any accidents. I believe everything happens for a reason. We may not know that reason, but it will eventually reveal itself. I believe our course is set from day one. Please remember from class one, I am a pessimist, and I am happy to follow the road, comfortable in my skin, and I will rest in peace or pieces if that's the case, and I refuse to be optimistic about that!"

Edmund was the last to join in the debate.

"The question from Peter was, does the fact that he and I have now come out change our genital stage? We are debating this question, and here is my opinion. It's very easy for me. We will all be judged (and in all honesty this is what we are talking about) by how much we are loved when our time comes. It's what you leave behind that counts, which Shakespeare said quite eloquently, 'the evil that men do live after them and the good is often interred within their bones.'

"I don't believe the changes we go through change our basics. We are wired how we are wired and reveal ourselves to ourselves, and indeed to others, when we are ready to do so. I do think big upheavals make us question things more deeply, as indeed they should do. We continue to change and grow until our final breath. Amen to that."

"And that, my lovely students, makes a perfect ending to this class. Number thirteen is next. Only seven to go to the end of this course. Your assignment for next time is to examine three words: id, ego and superego. And believe me, they are all different. Take your time, look deep inside, work out your insecurities, and where you may have an inflated view of yourself. Be very honest. Class dismissed."

Nobody socialised that evening; there was too much to think about. Suddenly class thirteen was at the door, and it was hungry like a wolf. They had all done their research and were ready to argue the toss.

Class 13

"Welcome back, boys and girls. Today we will attempt, and I say attempt because it is such a huge subject to take in, the id, the ego, and the superego. And to be quite honest I don't know if we can fit all three into one class. This subject is what really drew me to become a professor of psychology. I find these three opposing yet connected things fascinating and I still haven't figured it all out, but I do have my opinions. First let's take the id. This is instinctive and impulsive. We are born with it. Babies are nothing but pure unadulterated id. I myself have always believed that our personalities are stamped on us from day one. We have a source of bodily wants, needs, desires, emotional impulses, especially aggression and libido. And id acts according to the pleasure principle, immediate gratification, defined by the avoidance of pain. Freud believes id is unconscious. It has no judgement of value, no good, no evil, no morality… it just wants what it wants. I for one applaud the id for its simplicity. Thoughts on this, anyone?"

Lillie put her hand up.

"Well, Professor, I agree with you, it's certainly a tempting way to live your life. Imagine being able to do exactly what you like, whenever you like, and not getting punished for it. Damn shame we must grow up. Sounds like heaven to me. Not a care in the world, and just 'enjoy'. Non-stop pleasure, the mind boggles."

Patricia spoke next.

"Yes, it is a wonderful concept, but we do have to grow up, we don't have a choice. And I believe those that do not grow up and take responsibility are the kind of people who cause all the real problems in this world. You cannot just reach out and take what you want. It is morally wrong and dangerous. So as nice as the id part of our psyche seems to be, it is just not realistic."

Professor Handover jumped in.

"Yes, Patricia, which brings us nicely and quickly to the ego, and we will be jumping back and forth between the three terms as we discuss this because they are all linked together. The ego's job is to be exactly that, realistic to the id's needs and desires and enable the person to regulate things, stopping immediate gratification, and trying to function in the real world. Can anyone of you give me an example of the ego controlling the id?"

Max looked serious for a moment. This was right down his alley.

"Well, I immediately went to a sexual example, being the selfish pessimist that I am. So, the id sees an attractive girl, the id wants to jump on her bones and do the dirty, yet the ego demands the id takes a back seat and tries to determine whether the recipient is welcoming the flirtation, and then making the proper gentlemanly moves at the right time. I would say the id is the more honest of the two."

"Thank you, Max, that is a good example of what we are talking about here, if not a little crude! Anyone else have something to add?"

Edmund, feeling confident about this discussion and his opinion of it, decided to join in.

"What about this: you're sitting in a long meeting, doodling on your notepad, trying to pay attention. Your stomach is growling, you're hungry, you want food NOW! The id demands immediate nourishment, like a baby with his bottle, the ego, a little older and wiser, suppresses the urge, puts on an interested face, and waits patiently till it's all over. Then he goes to eat. It seems to me like the ego in all of this is simply the growing up part of life. Taking responsibility for things. Living in the real world where you sometimes must wait for what you want. I must admit, this was a hard thing for me to learn and I didn't always succeed in controlling my id."

"Yes, Edmund, well said. The ego separates what is real and helps to diagnose our thought patterns so we can function. The ego is reason and common sense, in direct contrast to the id, which is passion unfettered. I want to throw out a question to you all. Do you think we have a choice about id and ego or is it just nature's way of growing up and becoming responsible adults?"

Penelope took her shot.

"If this is a necessary part of life that we all must go through, why then do we live in a world full of ugliness? There are wars caused by power crazed maniacs, starvation caused by greed, robberies, murders, child abuse, oh I could go on. My question is why this part of the population causes these kind of problems... what happen to their ego? Are they stuck in their id, or is their ego overinflated, and they believe that don't have to answer to anyone? Is this the definition of a psychopath? I know it's a big question, but it's something I have always wondered about. What went wrong with these individuals? And it makes me consider my future after this course is over. I would like to make this my area of study. The criminal mind. Why do some people take this turn in life?

"Big subject with me, but for the sake of this class, I will stop there."

Professor Handover leaned on his desk, took a deep breath, and decided to do a left turn on his plans for the remaining classes.

"No Penelope, you should not stop there. In fact, you've brought up a very interesting subject, the psychopathic personality. I would like to explore everyone's opinion about these individuals. It's always fascinated me too. And after all, this is a psychology course and what could be better than to dive down into the underbelly of human beings? Your assignment is to find a particular psychopath that interests you, serial killer, child abuser, murderer, whatever, and write an essay on them, explaining why you think they turned out the way they did. This is not an easy assignment, but I think it could be very revealing in how we all view these outcasts from society. Okay. off you go. Enjoy... or maybe don't enjoy."

Penelope was the first to walk out of the class. She didn't say goodbye to anyone, as she was preoccupied. She was excited about this because she had a lifelong obsession with trying to understand these types of people. It was wonderful that the professor was going to explore this subject as part of the course, just wonderful. Briefly she wondered why she was so fascinated, and just as quickly dismissed the question. She was. End of. And she knew exactly who she would choose. Her number one of serial killers, Ted Bundy. He was at the top of her macabre hit list. Her top of the flops.

It was a nice time of the year at college, not too hot, not too cold. Max, Patricia, Lillie, Penelope, Peter and Edmund were engrossed in this assignment, so nobody made any plans to meet up. Yet they did bump into each other ambling round the campus, and in the bar unexpectedly. The meetings were brief though, as they all had work to do. It seemed nobody wanted to communicate. All affairs were put on hold.

Class 14

All the students filed in with their essays ready. The room was filled with a dark expectation. It was kind of spooky. This was not going to be a pleasant discussion. They took their seats quietly, waiting for the professor to begin.

"Welcome, everybody. Who wants to begin? Penelope, how about you?"

"Okay. I don't know exactly why I have always been so fascinated with serial killers, but I have. I think, and this is open to discussion, that it is probably because I always try to find the point in their lives when they turned left, or right as the case may be, and followed the dark path. I mean, of course, some people are evil, but for many of these cases, there was a turning point that pushed them over the edge of respectability.

"I have chosen Ted Bundy. I have read numerous books about him, especially by Ann Rule, who was his friend when he worked on a helpline with her, before she knew what he was doing in real life. *The Stranger Beside Me* is one of the best, can't-put-it-down books I have ever read. Researching him in detail, I could not find a point that turned him, and believe me I have tried. He does not fit the profile in any way. Good looking, articulate, kind and intelligent. He is the exception to the rule. When you read serial killers 'profiles, most of them follow a similar pattern. He does not… which to me, makes him irresistible. The updated book by Ann Rule of *The Stranger Beside Me* was very telling. Because they were friends, she took a very long time to be able to accept the fact that he was a murderer. She knew a different Ted. In her prologue to book two, she answers the question she was asked by most people, which she could not or would not answer previously. Was Ted Bundy evil?

"Yes, she was finally able to write. Wow. That really made me stop and think. My basic questions are, to all my classmates and to you Professor, do you think some people are born evil? And if so, was there no point earlier on in their lives that this could have been detected and dealt with or at the very least diagnosed? Are we all victims of society in one way or another or can we alter our course in life, no matter what ugly tragedies we are thrown to cope with?"

Like the aftermath of a bomb exploding, the silence was deafening.

"Wonderful questions, without easy, if any, answers. Let's examine this as we go through all the choices brought to this class today. Who's next?"

Patricia put her hand up." I'd like to go next please.

"I read a few books on the Moors murderers, Ian Brady and Myra Hindley, dubbed the most hated woman in Britain. We have all read the stories and reports. Shocking to the core. There is no need to go over their crimes again. The purpose of the exercise is why… so, cutting to the chase, there was no actual 'turning point ' for Ian as far as I could gather. He was described as quiet, punctual and short tempered. Exactly as the adult he became. He did torture and kill animals when young, which does seem to be a common thread amongst serial killers, and he was pushed from pillar to post, and never really knew who his dad was. This kind of unstable upbringing is also a common thread. And he had a fascination with the macabre, dwelling on atrocities during World War Two. Where his sexual deviation came from is not apparent.

"Myra Hindley is just plain confusing. Was she simply a victim of falling head over heels for the wrong guy? And together they became an evil force acting out each other's fantasies. It seems a shame they ever met. Myra learned early, from her father, that violence could be rewarded after she was attacked at school by a boy and her dad made her go back and retaliate. That I find interesting and very telling. She also said that Brady completed captivated her… 'Within months of meeting him Brady had me convinced there was no God at all. He could have told me the moon was made from green cheese and the earth was flat and I would have believed him. Such was the power of his persuasion.' Or

144

words to that effect. I did remember one quote from Myra's book that went something like this, 'you think I am abnormal, and people like me do not exist easily, well, I can tell you, we are your daughters, your sisters, we are amongst you.'

"Ian wanted his ashes to be spread on Saddleworth Moor, where the victims were buried, which I find particularly nauseating. My focus on these two is Myra. Was she already like this, a burning chink in her personality, or did her falling for Ian do the trick? It's a hard one to figure out. But if there is such a thing as 'normal', as a woman, Myra did not fit the bill whatsoever. Women serial killers are few and far between for all the obvious reasons. I find this subject very disturbing. Not to be sexist in anyway, I must say, women are NOT natural child killers. It goes against nature. We are nurturers after all. It's the way nature intended it. Very upsetting thought for me."

She sat back down with a very confused look on her face.

Professor Handover stood up quite aggressively. This was not an easy subject to try and teach or indeed to even direct the emotional and mental traffic. It seemed like everyone was identifying with their choices on some level. Oh well, he said to himself, over the cliff we go.

"I am not going to make this subject the focus of my course, but I must say, out of everything we have discussed and dissected in class thus far, this seems to be the most revealing, for many reasons, and may I add, the most disturbing. So... who is brave enough to go next?

Max was more than ready.

"I have chosen the irresistible couple (tongue firmly in cheek) of Fred and Rosemary West. The reason I have chosen them is that I do firmly believe that two halves can make a whole, whether it's healthy or not. Sometimes, like neutrons and protons, things come together and explode. Two incomplete people meeting and becoming one. Fred had indeed raped and murdered before. Fred was the second of six children. By his own admission, sexual abuse was common in his household. His dad had sex with his daughters, and bestiality even came into the picture at some point. Also, Fred was very close with his mother, who allegedly abused him from age twelve. It all fits the serial killer profile perfectly."

Max paused to let that thought sink in… he thought it was an interesting one.

"Rosemary had learning difficulties, with intellectual incapabilities, not very bright at all, and overweight. Not a good start in life. Her dad was a schizophrenic and sexually abused her. The road was paved with bad intentions leading her to her fate in life. She met Fred, who was twelve years her senior. Together they became a team, each completing the incomplete puzzle in each other. I have studied this and honestly have no idea who was the aggressor, the dominate evil. All I do know is that together they were an evil force to be reckoned with. My query is: are we all open to this kind of outcome? What separates us from these 'evil ' doers? Come on. Let's be honest here... couldn't a certain set of circumstances turn us around so we became one of these so called 'outcasts 'of society? Is there a killer buried somewhere inside in each one of us?"

Max breathed deep and heavy, then sat down with a loud thump.

"May I go next, please?" the exotic Lillie said softly, which was unusual for her, being such an upfront, plain-speaking person.

"I have chosen Charles Manson and his 'family'. We are all aware of the gruesomeness of these crimes. When I read my first book about the court cases, I had to put it down several times before I could pick it back up again and continue. It was that horrific. I have read much about his circumstances. He was in and out of prison for most of his life. It's one thing to be an evil character and make your fantasies of murder come true, it's another thing entirely to get other people to do it for you. He was clever and he chose wisely, preying on nice but neglected girls, many from affluent families, probably looking for attention, affection and a father figure. And they got all that in spades. He pulled the strings of everyone within his orbit. The hippie era, for Charles, was a perfect storm. Peace and love. Which in his reality translated into 'complete control'. After finally being released from prison he headed to LA, fancying himself to be a singer/songwriter, in the middle of the 'make love not war 'revolution. Took some LSD, liked it, took some more, gathered people around him so he could manipulate them, make them devoted to him, and could pour rubbish into their empty minds. In fact, he was a master manipulator. I could go on and on and on, as indeed his court case did. There seemed to be no end. But to top and tail it, what causes seemingly 'normal 'people to have a need to follow anyone to the extent they did? I don't question Charles. To me he was an accident waiting to happen. I do question those who blindly followed him. This is my focus.

"And, as a footnote, I have heard some of his compositions; one of them, originally titled 'Cease to Exist 'but changed to 'Never Learn Not to Love', became a Beach Boys B-side. Dennis Wilson was quite friendly with Charles and his family, they even moved into his house for a while, but he, thank goodness, saw the light and moved away to another home. Eventually the lease ran out and the Manson Family was kicked out. Dennis had simply distanced himself, sensing all was not kosher. Close call I would say. In my opinion, within this murderous spree you could do an entire analysis of human nature, at its best and its worst. As Patricia already pointed out, women are supposed to be nurturers… and once again, they were the perpetrators of the crimes, and the crimes were indeed heinous. And, since I am more interested in the female part of my choice, maybe what I am asking is, what turns a woman into a killer? Phew, now there's a question, eh?"

Peter piped up.

"Well, I am happy at the way these discussions are going because I have chosen a woman, few and far between though they may be. Aileen Wuornos. She shot seven men within twelve months, claiming it was all self-defence. She died by lethal injection.

"When I read up on her, she never had a chance. Not from day one. There was no element of 'normal 'in her life. A schizophrenic dad who committed suicide after being imprisoned for raping a seven-year-old. Abandoned along with her brother by their mother and left with their maternal grandparents who in fact were not their maternal grandparents. Poor Aileen was abused by her grandfather and had sex with her own brother. At eleven, she became sexual at school, in return for cigarettes, drugs and food. At fourteen she was pregnant after being raped by a family friend,

147

went to a home for unwed mothers, gave birth and had the baby adopted. Not a good start in life. By the time she was fifteen, she had left her family home, was living rough, and became a prostitute. No surprises there. What did she have to hang on to? Nothing.

"When you read about her life it is a series of tragedy after tragedy. No wonder she ended up hating human beings. And she did hate human beings. Make no mistake. Funny, thinking about that flip side that Manson wrote, 'never learn not to love'… Well, it seems like poor Aileen did 'learn not to love'. I say it again because it's unbelievable: seven men in twelve months, all shot multiple times. One of the last things she said was, 'Thanks a lot society, for railroading my ass.' I really wonder what she meant by that statement. Did she take no responsibility for her crimes? And if she didn't, I cannot blame her, seeing how so many crimes were committed against her as a human being. It is, sadly, understandable.

"I think this is not a case of being evil, in fact, it's a case of not being anything. She was used and abused her entire life and ended paying for it with her life. She had no chance whatsoever. Could anyone or anything have turned it around? I don't think so. It is a true tragedy. Out of our control. And that makes me very sad. I have nothing more to add except… poor woman."

Professor Handover decided to comment.

"Peter, food for thought. No need to answer immediately. Why do you think you chose a woman serial killer? I will leave that with you and indeed the rest of the class to analyse.

"Now, Edmund, it's up to you to finish our list of top ten serial killers. The 'hit man 'parade if you like." I'm so funny, he thought.

"Okay. I have chosen Jeffrey Dahmer, who murdered seventeen men and was known as the Milwaukee Cannibal. His murders included necrophilia, cannibalism and hoarding body parts. Like all the others we have discussed, he had a lot of problems in his early life. His mother was drug addict. She eventually left home with his younger sibling, leaving him alone to live with his father, who eventually remarried. He showed early signs of fascination with dissecting dead animals, with his dad's approval, who I am sure had no idea that this was leading to anything macabre. By the time he was in high school he realised he was homosexual. His dad, who was profoundly ignorant about what being gay meant, made him join the army to try and straighten him out, and eventually sent him to live with his grandmother, which in my opinion was a huge mistake. He basically washed his hands of him, although he did stay on the scene, visiting with his new wife. His dad seems a very interesting character. I wonder, did he have any idea what was going on? Did he not hear alarm bells going off? When you see photos of Jeffrey, he is most definitely not normal. Being a dad, he was most likely in denial.

"Jeffrey started his real killing spree after moving in with his grandmother, taking like-minded men home, drugging them, killing them, and doing whatever he did with the remains of them. His grandmother was totally unaware of what was going on under her nose.

"What I find interesting is not the actual killings themselves, as all serial killer stories are very similar, it's the fact that once he was behind bars in the Columbia Correctional Institution, he became a born-again Christian, or so he claimed. But herein lies the dichotomy. Months before he was beaten to death by a fellow inmate, he was questioning things. Am I sinning against God by staying alive? Interesting question. What do all you think? Was he sinning against God?

"In an interview he did for NBC he said, 'If a person doesn't think there is a God to be accountable to then what's the point of trying to modify your behaviour to keep it within an acceptable range? That was my thinking anyway.'

"And bringing it to the bitter end, after the first blow of the iron bar of Christopher Scarier, who killed him in the kitchen of the jailhouse, he said, 'I don't care if I live or die, go ahead, kill me.' He got his wish."

Edmund sat down with a thump.

Professor Handover let the silence settle. All six students sat quietly, digesting all the information.

"Well, where do we go from here? All your choices, explanations and questions were excellent. To be honest, I could do the whole course on this subject, but that is not why you're here.

You want to be well rounded thinkers, able to discuss all kinds of personalities, be objective and non-judgemental, but also have a decent working knowledge of what's what. This is a psychology course after all, and there must be no exclusions. Bringing serial killers into the equation, well, it simply had to be done.

"So, that's enough for today, more than enough in fact. There are only five more classes to go. Next week I would like you all to do a short essay on what each of you has discovered about human nature thus far. I am leaving it wide open for interpretation. Once you have all had your say, I will then make a concrete decision about the rest of the classes as we head towards the finish line. Well done everyone, well done indeed."

They all filed out looking a little relieved that this class was over. Even though it was interesting, it was unsettling at the same time, understandably. Time for a little R & R.

Max got together with Patricia, although a little reluctantly, as he was starting to feel his interest waning, Peter was with Edmund, still hot and heavy in the honeymoon period, and Penelope with herself; good thing she liked her own company. A change was coming as they were getting closer to the finish line, and they could all feel it. Lillie hung back a little, till they had all left, for obvious reasons.

They sat together in the students 'chairs, side by side, comfortable in each other's presence. Lillie had something to say, and she was determined to say it, however difficult it may be; she was determined to be kind and to leave her bluntness for another day and indeed another person. She had reached that point in this affair, the point always reached so far in her life, when the relationship had nothing more to offer her and started to feel stifling. This was a lifelong love affliction that she had no control over. Also, she was becoming acutely aware of the age difference. She reached for his hand under the desk and held it lightly. His was warm, hers cold.

"You know, hey professor, oh wise one," Lillie said, upbeat and cheeky sounding, to take the sting out of what was coming, "I feel it's time we 'talk'. We are nearing the end of this course, not long to go before we all go our separate ways. Although we have had an intimate relationship for a while now, and I have enjoyed it, we have not talked whatsoever about our future, if indeed we have one. I have been edging towards the negative for some time now, but in all honesty, I figured the relationship would run its course and dwindle out naturally so this discussion would be unnecessary. I now see that this is not going to happen. In fact, if I may be so bold, I believe you have allowed yourself to fall in love with me. I, however, am not in love with you. Sorry."

There. It was said. Plainly, simply and honestly, and very bluntly.

Although this was not a surprise, Professor Handover being a realist all the way, it was still somehow unexpected. Her words hung in the air like a bad smell. For a man who never committed to anyone, liked his own company, liked his job, liked his life, the heartbreak he was feeling shook him to his core. My God, he thought, how the hell did this happen to me, of all people. And for once he didn't think he was funny. He sat there for a few moments, looking at the floor, afraid to look into her eyes in case she saw how needy he had become. He tried hard to gather his strength and put on devil-may-care expression on his face. Then he thought better of it.

Why do I need to pretend? he thought. What do I need to prove and to whom, and what for? Damn. If ever there was a time to reveal me, that time is now. What have I got to lose? Nothing except my dignity, and to be honest, is that worth saving if it's built on sand? Okay... here I go over the emotional edge.

"Lillie. My sweet exotic Lillie, who brought me back to life. I was dead but had no idea I was. You have awakened my feelings, feelings I never knew I had. Depths I never realised I could reach. Happiness I didn't know was missing. You have given me a reason to exist beyond my existence such as it was, and now you want to remove yourself from me? And I am aware that this is pathetic emotional blackmail to use but I can't help myself."

Lillie stared into his eyes, looking very bewildered by this declaration. In her opinion, she had given him very little besides sex. Wow... what a turn up for the books this was. Talk about different perspectives!

He looked directly into her eyes as tears dripped down his cheeks. He was going for broke. He was collapsing, emotionally, physically and mentally, and had no power to stop it happening. He had given his power to her. He had opened his heart; he had let her in. Nobody had ever gone so deep inside before. And somewhere he knew that her getting in deep was nothing to do with her, but to do with himself. He wanted this experience. What a revelation that was. And you call yourself a psychology teacher, he thought to himself, quickly followed by, God, I am funny. Which somehow made it almost bearable.

"Is there anything I can do, anything I can say to make you change your mind? I won't lie, you are correct, I fell in love with you, and I don't know if it's possible to fall back out without doing serious damage. And at my age, that's not healthy. Funny, I always figured I would die quietly in my sleep. I never considered the possibility that it would be from a broken heart. I don't know what to do. Help me."

Lillie looked straight into his eyes, taking it all in, trying to find the right words, diplomacy not one of her strong suits. Be kind, be kind, be kind, she repeated to herself like a mantra, but mantras never did sit easy with her.

"Wow, I don't know what to say to you. You are piling on the guilt here, big time. This is not a load I want to carry around with me. I have my own baggage. I don't need yours too. The truth is, there is nothing you can do to fix this. I am not in love with you, and I am not going to fall in love with you, not now, not ever. Our romance has run its course. I am sorry, truly."

She gave her emotion permission to show itself, which was not comfortable but necessary in this situation.

She let go of his hand, kissed him on his wet left cheek, arose, straightened her back, and walk slowly out of the classroom.

"Ding," shouted the Professor after her, "that concludes today's lesson." God, I am funny, he thought to himself. Then why am I not laughing?

The poor man sat there, staring into space, numb. I must use my skills here, he said to himself. This is what I do, discuss and analyse people's psyches. I teach them how to survive life's pitfalls. How to not go over the edge. How to deal with whatever comes their way. When bad things happen, there are lessons to be learned. I am a professor of psychology, for God's sake.

He stood up, did a little emotional shiver, put the papers on his desk in order, got his coat and hat, wrapped the scarf around his neck, switched off the light and locked the door. He slowly walked back to his apartment, deep in his own little world, more alone than he had ever been in his entire life.

Max and Patricia were sitting quietly having a drink at what had become by now all the students' local. The atmosphere was heavy between them somehow, but you couldn't put your finger on it. Max sat there with his whiskey, Patricia with her G & T, sipping quietly, both inside their private thoughts. She was wondering if Max wanted to call it quits and was desperately hoping he wasn't. Although she was not in love, she was in like, which could turn into love of course, given time, which was not on their side. She decided to let him speak first. And after another silent fifteen minutes had passed, he did just that. She shrugged her shoulders in preparation.

"Look Patricia, I don't quite know how to put this, so I am just going to blurt it out.

"I have enjoyed your company mainly because you are the opposite of me, and the journey has been educational, for want of a better word. I am a lone wolf, always have been. To be honest, we have had an affair, that's all. Nothing more. I now want this affair to end because it is time for it to end. I feel it. I do want to say though, you have given me honest emotion and taught me that I do have the capability inside of me to fall in love, it's just not going to be with you. I don't want to hurt you, not at all. I do understand how vulnerable you are, it's what drew me to you, and that I am yet again another lover who is walking away. My advice would be, take what we have shared, keep the memories safe inside, stand tall and keep on walking. But the next time, try to walk towards somebody who will return your kind of unconditional love.

"You're a lovely person, and I am happy that you came into my life."

For Max this was a big step forward in expressing his emotions, which were usually locked inside, with no key to open them. He felt he owed her that much. Isn't life strange, he thought to himself.

Patricia did not collapse, did not break into tears, did not cause a scene; after all, she had been through this her entire life, this was just another chapter in her long running series of heartbreaks. She thought for a few more minutes before answering.

The minutes passed like hours… tick tock, tick tock, tick tock.

"Okay, Max. I understand and I accept. Just for the record, I am not in love with you, not yet anyway. Yes, we are different, and your maleness is what drew me to you.

"And, of course, repeating my pattern. I appreciate how you have said what you have to say. It was uncharacteristically kind of you. I would like to think that it was me who opened that avenue. I don't see why we should drag this out. We are both on the same page. I am going to leave now. I need to be alone to process."

She got up, leaving her unfinished drink on the table, with pink lipstick staining the glass, headed toward the door, stopped, turned around and said, "One more favour I will do for you, Max. Check out Penelope. I saw the attraction on the very first day. In my opinion you guys are made for each other. Good night, and goodbye. "

Peter and Edmund spent a quiet weekend, both busy with their essays. In a strange way they had become a little distant from each other in the last few weeks. Having bit the bullet and gone into a full affair, they had both mentally taken a step back to have a look at the situation. Cautious but wise.

Penelope spent the weekend alone. What choice did she have? She had a very strong feeling though that Max and Patricia would soon be uncoupled, so to speak. She had caught a look in Max's eye at the last class meeting. Definitely a 'got to get out of here 'kind of look, if her instincts were correct, and they were rarely incorrect. Let's see, she thought to herself, and continued with her essay; let's see, she thought, optimistically, which was her way.

Class 15

Penelope, Max, Patricia, Peter, Lillie, Edmund and Peter quietly filed in and took what were by now their normal places at the six neatly arranged desks, all in a row across the room. Professor Handover leaned on his desk, looking a little worse for wear, but determined to be professional and conduct the class to the highest level.

Brushing his feelings aside with a determined mental shrug, he rose up to his full height of 6 '1" and began.

"Good morning, students. Today is what I call a recap day. I asked you all to do a short essay about what you have learned so far. I am sure this will be interesting for the reader, and the listeners. And there will be a surprise guest essay reading at the end. So, which brave soul is going to go first?"

Penelope raised her hand, stood up with her pad of paper, cutely perched her glasses on her nose, and began to read.

"What have I learned thus far? I had to think long and hard about this. But the longer I thought about things, overthinking perhaps, moralising, digging too deep, philosophising, judging, I was wandering back and forth over old ground, trying to make sense of my life, the wins and the losses. Then, I stopped thinking, and started to use my feelings instead, and the words flowed out like lava.

"I have learned that although there are always two sides to every story, there is only one side that is right for you. This does not mean you're right, of course. Not at all. It is simply your perception, which we all have the right to. Our truth, if you like. I have learned to keep my channels open and to not judge too quickly, which I always have had a habit of doing, mainly because I believe my instincts are infallible. I have learned that each one of us, despite appearances, has buried treasures to discover. But, most importantly, I have learned that although I do like being alone, I really would like a partner now." She paused and glanced at Max without meaning to. "I feel like it is finally time to take my life in a new direction. This course has given me a new 'course 'to follow, a new understanding, not just of psychology, but of myself.

"The end... or possibly, the beginning."

There was a small ripple of applause from the rest of her classmates, and surprisingly, the professor.

A few minutes passed quietly, as the class digested Penelope's essay.

Max didn't raise his hand, he just stood up and started to speak, as was his way.

"I have learned a lot from these classes, in fact, more than I thought was ever possible for a guy like me. I have found every class interesting and informative, and... thought provoking. Many a night I have laid in my room thinking things through. Analysing, justifying, every which way-ing, still trying to stubbornly hold on to 'me', whoever the hell that is. I loved the id and ego stuff. It made complete sense to me and explained a lot of my character traits. I loved the 'triggers 'class, which for me was the most difficult, because I am not one to share these kinds of things. But the one thing that I am most grateful for is, and I must thank Patricia for this: I do have the ability to fall in love. She has given me that awareness, even though we are not a couple anymore as of last weekend. And, although it was at my instigation, I do believe the split is amicable." Max gave Patricia a soft smile, checking if she was okay with this revelation. She was, thank goodness. "And Professor, we haven't touched on the superego yet."

"Thank you for that Max; I am aware, and will get to it, probably in the next class. But saying that, the id and ego are the most important and we've done them."

Max continued, "I want to thank all of you for sharing and allowing me to be daring and, dare I say it, caring. That's it. The rest of my life, bring it on!"

"Thank you, Penelope, thank you, Max. Neither of you has disappointed me. In fact, you have lived up to my expectations. Miss Lillie, I sense this would be a perfect time to hear your essay."

This was extremely brave for Professor Friedrich Handover, but he couldn't bear to wait anymore, and quite possibly there was a little hint of revenge mixed in. Let's see what she has to say now, he thought. Let's see if she's even in the slightest bit sorry or ashamed. Yes, let's see.

Lillie began to speak.

"Well, after that last announcement, I would like to start with one of my own. The professor and I have also broken it off, last weekend. Must have been something these classes brought on, who knows. Anyway, that's how it is."

She stood silently for a few seconds, briefly glancing up at Friedrich Handover. She saw the pain in his eyes, as did the rest of the students, and looked down at her notes, a little uncomfortable but confident, straightened her back, and continued.

"I have enjoyed all these classes. They have given me insights into things I never had much time for. As we all understand each other quite well now, you know that I can be a cold fish, disguised as exotic, intelligent, challenging, whatever adjective you choose... I am cold. Guilty as charged. I think when emotions were handed out, I was at the end of the queue. For me the most memorable class was 'facing our demons'. That meant I had to unlock my heart, which I did, and I have had a damn good look inside. Most revealing and most valuable, and very surprising. I enjoyed the 'serial killers 'classes very much. I am like Penelope. Fascinated with the paths their lives took. I don't know what is coming next but am looking forward to the journey. I am feeling more fulfilled, more open to change, less judgmental, and ready for the next chapter of my life. As far as falling in love, the jury is still out on that one. But let's see. The door to my heart is not locked anymore, but it's not yet open. Maybe someone out there will have the key. Who knows? Four more classes to go. Anything can happen. I have enjoyed all your company so far, and that includes you, Professor. Especially you," she added, taking out the sting. "Thank you all for helping me to examine my idiosyncrasies."

Lillie exotically sat down. The professor was left unsatisfied intellectually and emotionally. It felt like foreplay without the sex. Oh well. So be it.

Peter and Edmund exchanged glances. Edmund knew Peter expected him to go first. So he did.

"I guess it's my turn. In all honesty, before I took this course I wondered if it was ever going to be my turn. I too liked the 'triggers' discussion. It had a double edge: not only do you have to identify your triggers, but you also need to go inside and find the origin. This was the real interesting point for me. I don't think I ever would have remembered being raped if these classes had not forced my mind back into dark, hidden corners. I am forever grateful for that. The id, ego, and yet to come, superego also made me stop and think. Why am I like I am? Also, do I need to have a reason why I am like I am? Do I need to justify myself? All in all, I feel like I have been making good headway here. I guess the biggest step I made was coming out. Isn't it funny how many hang-ups you can keep in a closet! I don't know what the future holds, I don't know if Peter and I will stay together. What I do know is that I feel ready, willing and able to take whatever life throws at me from here on in. I have learned to let go of my anger. I can honestly say, hand on my heart, I forgive my mom and so-called dad, totally. And what a relief that is. So freeing. So, thank you, every one of you. I could not have done this without all your input and your teaching, Professor. I never felt so close to a group of people in my life, dare I say it, you feel like family to me." A single tear rolled down his cheek. "And thank you, Peter, for taking a chance on me. That's about it for now. I say, hesitantly, there will be more revelations to come."

Patricia was more than ready to speak; boy oh boy, did she have a lot to say.

"What has this course taught me so far? It has shown me how I have allowed myself to be an emotional dumping ground for inadequate men who have no idea of what love and commitment means. I've been a trash can most of my life. It has taught me I have allowed this to happen, time and time again, because it's all I know. There is comfort in patterns, the devil you know and all that rot. It has taught me that I now must try and delete this pattern from my repertoire. I can't pick a favourite class or subject. I have enjoyed every single one of them, so far. And every single one has taught me something. And this weekend of being dumped, as Max so kindly informed you all. Which was fine, well, kind of fine with me. Not totally unexpected. After we split, I spent the rest of the time in my room working on this essay. And I am happy to announce, I have finally developed a set of balls; big ones too. And that, as far as I am concerned, is a result. If I get nothing else from this course, that's enough for me.

"Thank you everyone."

Patricia sat down heavily, with attitude, and a small smirk on her face.

"And now you, Peter, the last man standing."

"Okay… the class clown, the one liner king, never at a loss for words, is about to bare his soul. I have discovered that my whole life, whenever things got emotionally tricky, I reverted to comedy. Laugh so you don't cry, never the opposite way around, although maybe that would have been more honest of me. Seems to be that being amusing was my survival kit. This course has showed me that I don't have to make everyone laugh all the time. I don't have to make myself laugh. It's okay to feel whatever you are feeling. In fact, it's healthy. Better than bottling it up. I too liked the id, and the ego: very interesting stuff. I also enjoyed all of us saying what we thought psychology is. All very revealing. I am now ready to discover the serious part of myself. Once I have done that successfully, I can go back to Mr. Funny. Or maybe not. Maybe I will discover that I am quite a serious person underneath this forever smiling exterior. It's going to be one hell of a journey. And as far as Edmund and I go, I think we will both agree, we came together at the right time. Neither of us is possessive; what will be will be. Not ready to stop, still enjoying the honeymoon period. I just don't know if we will both be the same people when these courses are over, and we graduate to the next level. I have no idea what the future holds, but at least I know it holds something. Food for thought." Peter sat down.

"Thank you, each one of you. I am very proud of how far you have all come, how much you have shared, and how much you have all discovered about yourselves. I promised you a guest speaker, so…" Everyone turned towards the door, expecting somebody to walk in.

"… it's me! After this weekend's disappointment, I decided to write my own essay about what I've learned so far. Even though I am teaching this course, you're never too old to learn. As I have been taking you through your paces, discussing the ins and outs of psychology, I have had cause to question my own opinions. Watching you all break open and expose yourselves, whether you meant to or not, was a real eye opener for me, and a real heart-opener. As we have progressed, I found it harder and harder to be just the teacher, objective and not involved emotionally. And that's what I am. I am totally involved. I don't know if that's a good thing or not. There should be some distance between student and teacher." He looked pointedly at Lillie. "The lines should not be blurred, but blurred they are. I wanted to say my little piece now so that you would all be aware that you have all touched me, deeply. I care about what you learn from these classes, I care about what you do with what you've learned from these classes, and I care about where you go from here. I have one request. Please be gentle with me, I am an emotional virgin.

"And that concludes today's lesson."

Everyone clapped spontaneously.

"Class sixteen next. First we will cover the remaining superego, and then we will talk about basic personality types. You can all do some research on this. Are you open, are you closed, are you both? Do we fall into a natural pattern, or does upbringing and circumstance play a part? Have fun."

Class 16

It was confusing weather, the sun teasing itself in and out between the clouds, making it difficult to know how to dress for the day. The students arrived in various outfits to cover any eventuality, shirts tied round the waist, parkas, sweaters thrown over the shoulder, even a couple of scarves for good measure. They made their way to class, ready and eager to begin.

"So, my dear students, only four more classes to go, doesn't seem possible. It has literally flown by. Let's get started with superego, which plays the critical role in our psyches.

"Freud writes that superego operates on the morality principle and motivates us to behave in a morally acceptable manner. It is a part of the unconscious that is the voice on the conscience (doing what is right). It is the source of self-criticism. Basically, it makes us strive for perfection. Which is course is not possible. We can but try. This process starts way back with the id, then to the ego, and is influenced as we grow up by our parents, teachers, and anyone else we find inspiring. It's a coming together of all our knowledge and experiences thus far. Any thoughts on this?"

Max, dressed in his usual blue jeans and t-shirt, with surprisingly, and out a character, a sweater tied around his shoulders, looking more and more like a student every day, stood up without hesitation.

"Okay, Professor, interesting. I have a question. Is Freud saying that we are not moral people until this stage takes over, and is it a matter of taking over and being in control, or just the journey we all take as adults? Are we always adults when we get there or do some of us arrive at the superego destination early?"

Penelope was fidgeting in her seat, pulling on her hair, twiddling her thumbs, tapping her foot, anxious to speak, so she did.

"Can I just snowball on Max's comments? If the superego plays a critical role, how does it know when it has arrived at this illusive perfection?"

Edmund was fidgeting too, dressed oh so casually in slacks and a white shirt with stripes on it.

"Yes, what a puzzle this superego is. If this is the final stage of development, what happens if we don't get there, if we remain stuck in our ego phase? Is this a disaster? Can we survive this world? Does this make us immoral somehow?"

"All good questions. Max, to address yours, I don't think we are immoral, but rather developing our final moral credo. We all have done things we aren't proud of. Hopefully we learn from our mistakes, and that becomes a part of the superego's destination. And if indeed some of us get there early, all I can say is well done. Pat yourself on the back and enjoy the rest of your life.

"Penelope, you raise an interesting issue. The very word 'criticism 'denotes not being perfect but that is what the superego is striving for, and it is a conundrum. I guess we must trust ourselves and our very own superegos that once our train has arrived, we will get on board with it, hopefully with a first-class one-way ticket.

"And Edmund, over to you. I do believe this is personal. I am not being judgemental whatsoever when I say it's hard to make the decision to 'come out 'anyway, and you did leave it for quite a while, so I would question your own feelings about how you feel about who you are. My advice would be, to banish any negative thoughts from your heart and soul. You are who you are. Loud and proud. You're a valuable human being. If you remain in the ego phase, I don't think the superego will miss just one person!

"Okay. Your next assignment will be personality types. In 1928, Marston published a book about the emotions of 'normal ' people and had four different classifications known as DISC. That's all I am going to say. I would like you all to study this and be prepared to discuss it in detail both subjectively and objectively. Good luck, it's a complicated one."

162

The students filed out, quiet and thoughtful, on what turned out to be an Indian summer kind of day. Sweaters were removed and tied around waists, and jackets were shoved in their backpacks, along with their notes and books. There was an awareness that this course would soon be ending and that they all needed and wanted to get to the finish line. Max sped up a little and tapped Penelope on the shoulder. She was startled, as she was deep in thought, but not unhappy with the intrusion. Quite the opposite.

"Hi Pen, how ya 'doing? Seems ages since we've spent any time together. How about a drink this evening? I would like to kick some thoughts around with you."

Penelope paused, brushed a stray piece of hair from her cute face, opened her big hazel eyes wide, and just short of fluttering her eyelashes replied, "Sure. Meet me at the normal bar at 8:00 p.m. and bring your brain with you."

Edmund and Peter strolled off together, nearly holding hands but not quite certain if they should or not, so they erred on the side of caution, and walked slowly, close together, brushing shoulders now and again. To the astute observer, their relationship was obvious.

Patricia was daydreaming and banged into Lillie, knocking her school paraphernalia out of her hands. Lillie was not daydreaming as such but was definitely preoccupied.

"Whoops... sorry, Lillie. Here, let me help you pick up your things. What a jerk. I was a million miles away."

"No problem, Patricia. I do believe that there are no accidents. Why don't you and I meet up for coffee? We can discuss our breakups in detail. Maybe there is something to learn. How about it? Are you game?"

The student bar was busy but not uncomfortably so. Max and Penelope found a cozy little spot for two, sat down ordered a couple of G & Ts. Max talked first.

"Well, I don't know about you, but I am fascinated with this DISC thing. I think it will answer a lot of questions, about who we are, and our fellow students. I can't wait to get stuck in tomorrow."

"Me too, Max, but I have a feeling this is not why you asked me out for a drink tonight."

"No, it's not," he said, staring her straight in the eyes, openly, honestly, and surprisingly, looking vulnerable... a new colour for him. "I want to talk about you and me. I am now unattached, as you know. Was never attached in the first place, just dating. I am never very good with skirting around issues, so I will just say it straight. I would like to go out with you. We were attracted from day one, then I took a sidestep and 'we' got put on the back burner. How about it. You in or out?"

They sipped their drinks. Penelope was enjoying his discomfort and determined to draw this out for a long as possible, without making it obvious.

"Okay, Max. My response to your suggestion is, I am open to dating you, and yes, the attraction was always there. I have just one question though before it's a definite go. You chose Patricia instead of me. She is needy, clingy, and not your type whatsoever. I saw it happening, so I did take a back seat. I must admit, I knew it would not last. I just need to know why her instead of me, and why me now?"

They sipped their drinks again. This was not an easy conversation to be having; it was uncomfortable for both of them. But if there was to be a positive outcome, these questions had to be answered. Max went up and got them two more drinks. They both needed them!

"Okay, here I go. I will not overthink anything. I will let my words do the talking.

"Patricia attracted me because she *was* so clingy. It makes a man feel powerful to be needed so badly. For the short time we saw each other I enjoyed this ego trip, which is all it was. I must say though, to be fair to her, she did show me that I am capable of being nice to the opposite sex, caring, loving, and protective. Qualities I never thought I possessed. I do and did thank her for that. But finally, this need in me came to an end, and I began to feel claustrophobic. I had to get out. That is the answer to question number one. Question number two, why you? It seems to me that we are very similar characters, loners, intelligent with an awareness of who we are, above and beyond the rest of the students. I hope this doesn't sound big headed. It is my observation.

If Patricia hadn't waylaid me with her sweetness, you and I would have been an item from day one."

"Okay, Max. My answer is yes. Cheers."

They clinked glasses, paid the bill and left the bar, holding hands for the first time, walking towards their destiny.

Lillie and Patricia ended up in the library studying DISC together and drinking their café lattes, debating on which personality types each of their fellow students were, and indeed who they were. Two very unlikely candidates were becoming friends, as if it was meant to be all along. Two opposites finding they had a lot more in common than they realised.

Max and Penelope, although agreeing to see each other, were not quite ready to leap into bed, although the desire was there. Slowly was the key word here.

Edmund and Peter spent the evening together, having gotten out the appropriate reading material from the school library. Unlike Lillie and Patricia, they did not discuss their findings. They sat in silence making notes for the next class meeting.

And finally, it was class seventeen.

Class 17 and 18

It was a crisp autumn morning as the usual suspects filed in. This time though, the seating arrangement was different. Max and Penelope sat together on one side, looking somehow as if they had a secret, Peter and Edmund sat in the middle, together yet separate, and Patricia and Lillie sat on the other side looking very comfortable with each other. If the professor noticed anything, he said nothing.

"Good morning, students. I hope you are fresh and fit and ready for today's discussion. DISC, which stands for the four personality types according to Marston's 1923 personality type book. I have read it in detail and will be paraphrasing what I have read and how it has translated to me. I may at many points quote directly from the book as I have written down certain sections because to be honest, I can't say it better.

"Let us name them.

"D is for Dominance. These people are bold and sceptical, they dive into challenges unafraid, and their aim is to win at any cost. They are receptive to logic, data and analysis, but not as a rule to gut feeling or for that matter intuition. Dynamic, assertive, self-assured, they can get annoyed with opposing views and become indifferent and most definitively intolerant. Sometimes even hostile.

"I is for Influence. These types are bold, accepting, and people orientated. Good communicators. For them it's all about the connection. They are warm, welcoming, with an air of excitement about them. They enthusiastically and optimistically can keep everyone around them happy. But they can be reluctant to give constructive feedback due to their feelgood needs within.

"S if for Steadfastness. This personality is cautiously accepting and highly motivated to maintain stability in their

166

environment. Keywords are cooperation, calm and patience. When challenges arise in their environment they will be thoughtful, and methodical, providing empathy and support. They do struggle with disruption of any kind to their routine and can become utterly useless in this situation.

"C if for Compliance. Cautious and sceptical, detail orientated, everything in order. They do enjoy showing expertise and quality in their work. They are logic and objective driven and will respond to descriptions in a routine question with a flexible verbally proposed way forward. They tend to over analyse until they reach a level of comfort. Then and only then can they be a good source of objective support.

"Let's begin by each of you simply telling me which personality type you think *you* are."

Penelope raised her hand enthusiastically. This subject appealed to her, big time.

She was wearing her favourite pink t-shirt, paired with her favourite faded blue jeans, her long brown hair pulled back into a ponytail, looking more like a teenager than a young adult attending college.

"I, for influence. That's me. I consider myself to be an excellent communicator, and people reader. I try not to judge and am accepting of all. I have big shoulders, and don't mind somebody leaning on them. And I give great advice because I listen. I am the eternal optimist, which brings us right back to the beginning of these classes. Full circle. Happy to say I am still me!"

Max smiled at Penelope in his slightly cocky way and added his two cents' worth.

"Well, to be honest there are bits of me in the entire DISC description but if I must choose one, I will say I am D for dominance. I do respond more to logic than gut feeling, always have, I do prefer to win, and I am not afraid to dive into the deep end, and yes, I do not like to be questioned, challenged, or argued with. I am a self-contained individual. And I still sit on the side of pessimism."

Edmund looked at Peter, silently signalling him to go next, which he did.

"My turn, I guess. I went over and over these descriptions trying to make up my mind. It was a little confusing for me as I don't really think I fit into any of these a hundred per cent. The one that has resonated the strongest with me, I guess, is S for steadfastness. Growing up in the family I did, I had no choice but to be accepting and to try and keep the peace. My way was to find humour in everything, whether it was funny or not. I found a routine that enabled me to get through my life up to this point, and it's true I do not like any disruption to this routine whatsoever. Over to you, Edmund."

"Peter and I studied together but we did not discuss anything at all. I guess we were alone with our thoughts. I believe my personality type is C for compliance. I am anally organised, everything in its proper place physically and emotionally. I don't like surprises of any kind. Because of my upbringing, not knowing who my father was, and all the emotional baggage that came with that, the only option for me was to over analyse until I felt comfortable with 'me'. The journey has not been easy, but here I am. Ta da!"

The two girls sitting together, looking like two peas in a pod, rose at the same time, which made everyone giggle. Patricia took the initiative and started to speak. Lillie sat back down.

"I would have to say the old Patricia would have been S for steadfastness. But for slightly different reasons than Peter, I was always welcoming, calm and patient, all my life, trying to establish a routine that worked for me. I was a door mat for a long time. But now, this new person that I feel I have become has developed balls at last, and not before time. This Patricia is C for compliance. I will be proud of my skills, and I will show them off if need be. And, as for analysis, I will continue down this new path until I find my comfort zone. I am ready for a new life, and I have this class and all of you to thank for that."

A small ripple of warm applause rang around the room. Lillie was ready to talk now.

"D for dominance, which fits me comfortably. I came into these classes sure of myself, and I still feel the same. I am not overly emotional, or sensitive. Love is still an elusive four letter word to me, but I am not bothered by that. I remain sceptical of most things but will listen to logic. I am dynamic and self-assured. I like me and feel like I am in a good place. If these classes have taught me anything it's that I am exactly who I always thought I was. "

Professor Handover stood up, pacing back and forth a few times, pausing to look at each student's face. Smiling and thoughtful, pleased with the progress they had all made together.

"Well, everyone, I think that's it for today. We have done DISC, or is it DISC that has done us, just for the record." He chuckled. "Class eighteen is next. Just for fun, I am going to ask you all to bring to class your thoughts on anything we may have missed. Any hidden corners we haven't hit upon. Dig deep and let's see where that takes us. Class dismissed."

There was the hustle and bustle of chairs being pushed in, and notepads stuffed into backpacks and handbags. Finality was in the air. An ending. Only two more classes to go, then they would all be freed to roam the planet with whatever they had gleaned from this course. It's fair to say that all six students were deep in thought, with serious looks on their faces. They said their goodbyes then went their separate ways. No socialising, there was work to do.

In a flash, it was time for class eighteen.

"Welcome to each one of you. This is an anything goes day. Loose and easy, no subject is banned. You are free to talk about whatever, wherever your psyche takes you. You can talk to the class, or you can talk to an individual. I am handing over the reins and in fact I'm going to join you and sit down. Today I am not the professor, I am just another human being trying to figure things out."

And he did just that. He left his desk, pulled out another desk and chair and sat down at the end of the row. He even loosened his tie!

"Who would like to start this day's festivities?"

There followed a pregnant pause as nobody wanted to be the first one to leap into this void called exposure.

"Shall I start then?" Professor Handover said softly, totally understanding their hesitance.

"Lately I have been contemplating my existence on the planet, wondering, for the first time in my life, how long I have left. I don't know what led me down this road, it is not my usual destination. I guess I must be feeling my age, which isn't a bad thing. After all, as my mother used to say, 'We are only sure of two things in this life, we are born, and then we die.' Wise woman. So, without being pessimistic, I am in fact looking at death. The Grim Reaper who comes to us all eventually. It could be that this has descended because of Lillie's and my breakup, and the depression this has created in my heart, which surprised me, and my soul, which I never actually believed in before now. I have opened myself up to pain, and I am facing it head on, not hiding from it. The fact that I can say these things, and more importantly share them with you, my dear students, says a lot about me. I may be the teacher, but I have also been taught."

"And that's my cue," said Lillie, sounding a little put out. "Okay, here it goes. I would like to publicly apologise to you, Professor. It was never my intention to hurt you even though I can be a cold fish at times. We were an interlude, a fling, a romance, never destined to be forever. Not as far as I was concerned anyway. And just to put the record straight, I think it's wonderful that I was able to help you locate your heart and your soul. This could be the missing link you have been looking for. As you said, this is an anything goes day, and I needed to address this issue. Please don't judge me harshly, any of you. I saw a chance for some fun and I took it. When it was time to go, I went. You're a good guy Friedrich, and I wish you nothing but happiness. And now for me, this subject is closed."

"Lillie, it's nice that you apologised but don't you think you're being unduly harsh? You could have softened that with a look, even a hug, a kiss on the cheek, whatever, instead of just delivering your closing remarks. It wouldn't do you any harm to find *your* heart and soul," Penelope strongly stated, surprising herself.

"No, I stand by what I said and exactly how I said it. Anything more would be leading him on, which I have no intention of doing. You, Penelope, of course, are entitled to your opinion."

"Hey, both of you, I am sitting right here and you're talking about me in the third person. Looks like this is turning into an emotional debate of sorts. Maybe *I* am the topic of discussion this week. I don't mind. Let's see where it takes us."

Patricia put a comforting arm around Lillie and gave her a little hug.

"To our surprise, Lillie and I have unexpectedly become friends these last couple of weeks. Not close yet, but the possibility is there. We have both had break ups and have found a lot of common ground. I feel like I should stick up for her.

"Lillie, I have found you to be a no-nonsense person. And I admire that. You always know where you stand with you. What you see is what you get. I don't think you were being harsh just now, just very honest, which is never a bad thing as far as I am concerned. I do hope some of your resilience rubs off on me."

Max was watching the drama play out, trying to decide if he should speak or not. Maybe best to ignore this hornets' nest for a few more minutes and see which way the tide turned.

Peter, who had been sitting quietly, listening and observing body language, felt he had to speak. His thoughts had been brewing for a few weeks now and he could contain them no longer.

"On the subject of love and romance, which seems to be what we are talking about today, there is no right or wrong. We all have our own way of dealing with these matters. Some of us wear our hearts on our sleeve, and some of us need to be in charge and control the situation. Some of us leave and some of us are left. Since we are having a 'let it all out 'kind of a day, I am going to take the spotlight off the professor for a moment and make an announcement of my own."

They all looked at Peter expectantly, wondering what on earth he was going to say, maybe that he was straight after all?

"Edmund, thank you for coming into my life and allowing me the opportunity and giving me a reason to come out. You have given me love, companionship, and comfort. And I am grateful for that. I do feel though that it is time for me to move on. No concrete reasons. It's just time. I realise you have been my introduction into this way of life, and I now feel the need to look further afield. I know this is probably not the time or place to make this declaration, but in a way it's a perfect opportunity since we are all being honest and throwing caution to the wind. Sorry. That's how it is."

Peter looked Edmund straight in the eye so there was no doubt about how he felt and gave him a big hug. It was a goodbye hug. An awkward moment for everyone, and completely unexpected, especially for Edmund, who had no idea whatsoever that this was coming.

"Obviously I am nonplussed, as you knew I would be, not because of what you have said, but saying it here publicly in front of our fellow students and teacher. I would like to be just as honest with you in return. My take on 'us 'is the following. We saw an opportunity. We took it. We ran with it. We played with it. We enjoyed it. Love never came into the equation. I too feel it is time to move on. Now that I have accepted one hundred per cent who I am, and I might add very proud to be who I am, I am more than ready to see what's around the corner."

Edmund looked Peter straight in the eye and gave him a hug back.

"Wow, you two," said Max. "That was quite an inspiring exchange of words. I am impressed. You two have managed to have an affair and end it amicably; what could be better? No blame, no shame and no regrets. I am curious though, do either of you think that this ability to be open and honest with each other was helped by what we have learned in this course? Because what I feel I am witnessing is the direct result of all the self-examination we have been doing. I do feel we have all come a long way. Patricia, I would like to say thank you. For being the kind and caring person you are. For showing me that I am capable of love, and for being a class act all the way when we broke up. And as far as you and your newly found balls, bravo! A long time coming. I hope you and I can remain friends when this is all over. You would be a great friend to have. And now that I am on a roll, I would like to make you all aware that Penelope and I are an item. We have not consummated the relationship yet, but I can assure you that will happen very soon. In case you didn't notice, we fancied each other from day one." Max looked fondly at Penelope with a twinkle in his eye. "And you Professor, you're okay. Aside from your rotten jokes, which are never funny, you're cool. I wonder if you will find someone to love now that you're wide open to the idea. I hope so. Truly. Lillie, stay as sweet as you're not! Seriously, you are who you are. Difficult maybe, but interesting, absolutely. I would like to say that I am very happy I took this course. I have learned a lot about myself and my place in this world. Thank you to each one of you."

For the first time in his life, Max felt humble and just a little tearful. It was not an unwelcome feeling, and it was long overdue.

"And that, my good people, is a perfect place to end our class today. What an inspiring hour it's been. Next time, class nineteen will be our final proper class. Class twenty will be our celebration day, champagne, cake, and whatever else we want to do. Maybe somebody can bring in some music. If you play guitar and have one, drag that in. I will see if I can get some of the staff to roll in that ancient piano from the gymnasium. Does anybody play piano?"

"I do," said Patricia. "Not very well, but good enough for a sing song."

"Your homework is the following: going full circle to the beginning of this course, I want you all to bring in what you would like written on your tombstone. Off you go. You have some serious thinking to do, and so do I. Class dismissed."

Max and Penelope walked out shoulder to shoulder, heads together in conversation.

"This is going to be challenging," whispered Penelope.

"It sure is," whispered Max back.

"What do you say we take a breather this weekend and totally concentrate on the job at hand, no pun intended. Why don't we agree to consummate this relationship after the party. Something to look forward to."

"Yep... I agree."

Edmund and Peter walked together in comfortable silence. They had both said their piece and were happy.

"Edmund, would you like to get a drink at the bar with me, and then retire to our separate rooms?"

"Peter, what a splendid idea. Lead the way."

Lillie and Patricia were strolling slowly across the front lawn of the college. It was such a pretty time of the year, with the autumn leaves strewn around in all their glorious colour.

"Patricia, how about we grab a quick bite to eat at the diner? Then, I want to spend my weekend alone. I am taking this assignment very seriously. It's all about how we want to be remembered. Nothing glib will do."

"I agree, Lillie. I too need my alone time."

The professor sat at the student desk for a little while, not in any hurry to go. He was thoughtful, as he replayed the conversations from the day's class. He must have sat there for a half an hour when he started to feel a little strange. He couldn't quite say why he felt strange, but he did. It was a feeling he had never had before. Something wasn't right. Feeling dizzy, he decided to go back to his apartment and take it easy. Climbing the stairs slowly, he let himself in, hung his coat on the rack, turned the heating up, grabbed a small whiskey, got a pen and paper, turned on the light and sat on his couch. "Damn, I wonder what's wrong with me?" He forced himself to be calm, hoping the whiskey would do its trick. No television, no radio, total silence while he contemplated his life and the words he would write for next week's class. Maybe I am just feeling my age, he thought again, for the second time that day.

"Well come on, Grim Reaper, if that's you knocking on my subconscious. Try ringing the bell, if it's the final round," he said aloud to his empty room.

Class 19

It was a cold, drizzly day; umbrellas and raincoats were called for. Students were hustling and bustling all over the campus trying to get to their various destinations before they got too wet. Penelope, Max, Patricia, Lillie, Edmund and Peter hurried up the cement path, went inside the classroom, shook off the rain, hung their coats over the back of the chairs and sat down quietly, waiting for this last lesson to begin. The professor arrived a little late, but only by six minutes, looking a little worse for wear. The class began.

"Good morning, students. I can see by your expressions that you're wondering if I am okay. Let me assure you I am fine. I did have a little wobble over the weekend, not drinking, just not feeling a hundred per cent.

"My entire course has been leading up to this day. None of you knew that I have always had a deep fascination for tombstones. I've always kept this little quirk private.

"Even as a child I would love to go into graveyards and read the inscriptions. I would imagine the person and the life they had led, the choices they had made, and if they died peacefully. I would especially like the nearly unreadable ones from the days of old, they had a special meaning for me, different times, different goals and ambitions. Just fascinating stuff. I still do this. I wander aimlessly around, lost in my world of dreams and regrets. I always feel very connected to those six feet under. You dig?" He smiled. "But today is not about me, my job is done here. Today is about all of you. My special six who have given me so much back, which I never expected. I shall be sorry to say goodbye to you all next week.

"Right. Enough from me."

Max took the plunge. He wanted to get his over with.

175

"I believe that our personalities are stamped on us from the day we are born. I believe that no matter what happens in our lives, we basically stay the same. That's both a comfort and a curse. I thought long and hard about this. I am not someone who runs off at the mouth. I wanted mine to be one hundred per cent truth. And, I must add, these words would not have been what I would have written on my tombstone before this course began, but they are now. Here is my inscription:

"Here lies Max Morose, arrogantly humble, and optimistically pessimistic. I WILL rest in peace. No flowers. Thank you."

Patricia felt it was right to go next, so she hesitantly stood up, looking as vulnerable as she did on the first very day of class. Silent sympathy could be felt around the room.

"I don't have any extra words to say on this matter, my headstone says it all:

"Here lies Patricia Hodges, who came, who saw, and eventually conquered. Though she never knew if she had won or lost, at least she played the game."

Reflective and thoughtful were the moods of the day, as each person's final words were digested.

Peter cleared his throat as he stood up, smartly dressed in black jeans paired with a white striped shirt, white socks and brown shoes with matching belt, with a definite spring in his step that hadn't been there before. He was willing and ready to share.

"Here lies Peter Pendergast, if life is nothing but a cosmic joke, this is one hell of a punchline." He paused for laughter. "Thank you all for coming, and good night."

"Excellent, everyone, truly," said the professor. "I am blown away by your insights, your understanding of yourselves, and how you have been able to contain it in your last few words, so to speak. Three more to go." He looked pointedly at Lillie.

Lillie was dressed in her most colourful outfit: floaty pink skirt, floral blouse and motorcycle boots. Her large, hooped earrings were on show, and quite a few beaded, jangly necklaces swished as she slowly got to her feet.

"I don't have a lot to say either but I do sincerely hope that once I am gone, I will be remembered with kindness. Coming to this conclusion over the weekend was a strange revelation for me, always being the type that danced to her own beat, sang her own song, lived her life by her rules, no compromises. So, here is mine, and it is meant to be tongue in cheek. I hope it translates as such. My small attempt at humour:

"Here lies Lillie Lawford; Independent and judgemental she may have been, but under that brash exterior was a brasher one, waiting to get out! Hey, you. Get off my grass."

A small ripple of laughter floated around the room, as they exchanged smiles with each other. The professor had a sad smile on his face. Lillie had put it there. Max glanced at Penelope sideways, trying to read her. For some reason, this was not easy today. It had always been easy before. Edmund was sitting straight and tall in his seat, glancing neither left nor right. He was in the moment and would not be moved.

"Well, I guess I am next," said Penelope, "as we seem to be alternating between boy and girl, always the best seating arrangement. I share this love of graveyards with you, Professor, and my reasons are basically the same except for one point. I always try to work out what those bodies lying below didn't get in their lives. If they didn't find peace, what regrets they carried to the end, if they loved, if they lost. Basically, if they were happy when their time ran out. There were many scenarios to imagine for an imaginative girl like me. Every now and again I would come across one that stopped me 'dead '(pun intended) in my tracks, something that seemed like a perfect life, which of course nobody gets. Anyway, I digress, here's mine.

"Here lies Penelope Perfect, always sure of who she was, always had all the answers, always told the truth. The truth is, she died pessimistically optimistic!"

Max and Pen looked directly at one another. There was a 'tonight's the night 'look in their eyes. And not before time.

Not wasting a moment, Edmund abruptly stood up, anxious to get this over with.

"The universe has decreed that I will be the final speaker, which is fitting as this is how my life has always been. I am not playing the victim here; I accept my position one hundred percent. Before I wrote my words, I thought about whether I was happy with who I am, what I have accomplished, what I hope to achieve, tried to imagine my future life and where it may possibly take me. Will I find love, or better yet, will it find me, and if it does, will I be brave enough to open the door? Will I have children? And before you ask, yes, I do want children, always have. Will I be happy to let go, when it's my turn?

"Here lies Edmund P. Woodhouse. I lived, I loved, I laughed, I cried, then I died. Now, I don't have to hide."

"Give yourselves a round of applause. Well thought out, well presented. I am beyond pleased with the journey we have all taken together. I too have written my inscription and will read it next week at the start of our end of course party. Have a great weekend, everyone."

Everyone filed out, subdued but not unfriendly. This was a heavy subject, and nobody took it lightly. In writing their tombstone inscriptions they had exposed the deepest part of themselves. Not that they hadn't been doing this all along during this entire course. But this was the end of the journey… truly. Hard to believe that they would all go their separate ways after next week's party. They decided to go together to their local bar for a drink. A mental unwind was needed. They arrived and found a table suitable for six people and sat down. Edmund offered to buy the first round. They all ordered. While waiting for their tipples, conversation started up in dribs and drabs. They were all happy to let it fall where it may. They were all mentally both stimulated and exhausted.

Peter turned to Lillie, wanting to engage with her.

"I thought your inscription was great. You said exactly what you wanted to say with the minimum number of words. Can I ask you a rather personal question?"

"Of course you can. Nothing I like more than a full frontal attack," she replied, winking seductively, but with a lot of cheek.

"Even though you stood up in class and said how you feel, and that you had no guilt about the professor, I sense something different. I think you do feel a little bad about it. So, I am asking you, one to one, with no one else listening."

Lillie looked around her to make sure there was no eavesdropping, reddened slightly and answered Peter's very perceptive question.

"Yes, in my hidden corners that I usually keep on the top shelf shoved right to the back, I do feel sorry for him. Not because of the fling itself, but because he has never loved anyone. And I knew this before we began, but I let it begin anyway. It's not something I am proud of. And, quid pro quo, can I ask you a personal question?"

"Of course."

"Why did you break it off with Edmund? What was it that he was not providing you with? Now here is my amateur psychology coming to the fore. I think, perhaps, you are wondering if you may be straight after all. Correct me if I am wrong, but didn't you have a little crush on me to begin with? No bullshit now!"

"Okay Lillie, no bullshit… yes, I did like you, a lot. I started to examine your attributes, and I mean your strength of mind, which I found very attractive, then I began to wonder why I was going down that straight road, when the curved one was just to the left. I had sensed that Edmund was this way inclined, and I always knew I could swing either way. And you were otherwise engaged anyway. I did see you leave the classroom with the professor that first time and it was obvious. In the end, this experienced beckoned and I thought, why not. But I can't say I know where I go from here. I am just going to follow my road wherever it leads me."

All conversation stopped for a minute as Edmund arrived with all the drinks on a tray. Two G & Ts for Max and Penelope, who were huddled close together, a glass of Chardonnay for Patricia with ice, a glass of Merlot for Lillie, and a nice big pint of beer for Peter. Edmund had the same.

Edmund turned to Patricia and said "Cheers" and they clinked glasses. "To the sweetest, most vulnerable person I have ever known. Don't ever change, girl, don't you ever change. With balls or without, I like you just as you are. It's a shame I bat for the other team, or you and I would be an item."

He was not expecting that outburst to come out and was quite embarrassed by it even though it was the truth. Well, he thought, that's what these lessons were all about, weren't they?

179

Patricia skirted past it, sipping her drink, letting the awkward moment pass.

"Edmund, I will tell you what touched me about what you had to say. You want children. Do you know how important that is, that you could even admit to that? It struck me so hard and so deep. You must make this a reality; however it is possible. You would make a terrific father. And thank you for your compliment. I will treasure that."

Max and Penelope were exchanging thoughts, both trying to guess whose bed it would happen in.

"Max, I loved listening to you today. I am going to go out on the limb here emotionally to say that you are everything I thought you were from the first time I laid eyes on you. Arrogant and humble, exactly as you said. I find you very interesting, besides the sexual attraction which is obvious."

"Pen, let's finish these drinks and get the hell out of here. I honestly cannot wait anymore."

"That sounds like a plan, Max."

Max and Pen said their goodbyes about fifteen minutes later and made their way to Penelope's apartment. She wanted to be on familiar ground. Peter and Lillie walked out together, parting ways to their separate digs. Edmund and Patricia had a little hug and said goodnight.

On the other side of the campus, Professor Handover was on his couch, as alone as alone could be. He was staring at the words he had written over the weekend. His usual shot of whiskey was on the table. He gulped it down, waiting for the nice feeling that usually accompanied it, but instead he started to feel unwell. His heart started to race and then it started to hurt. Right across his chest it was very painful. He was short of breath and clutching at the air trying to shove in more oxygen. He tried with everything in him to calm down, but it was impossible. He was petrified. He knew he was having a heart attack. He turned very pale and fell to the floor, hitting his head on the coffee table. His tombstone inscription landed on the ground, face up. He landed on the ground, face down.

Class 20

Max and Penelope took their seats, both looking like the cat that got the cream. The deed was done and by the looks of it successfully. The rest sauntered in. They were all very curious as to what the professor's tombstone would say.

Just then a policeman came into the classroom door, accompanied by a frail, sad looking old woman of about eighty years old. She was white haired, and conservatively dressed. He was holding her arm, leading her carefully to the front of the classroom. She walked slowly, carefully, with dignity, as straight backed as she could manage.

"What the hell is going on?" said Lillie, who was the only who had found her voice.

He was a tall cop, about thirty years old, a badge, belt, holstered gun on the side, gleaming and shining, looking every inch of his profession. Nice looking, grey eyes and sandy hair underneath his hat. He did not look happy. He looked uncomfortable. But this was his job. He pulled out a chair and gently sat the lady down.

You could hear a pin drop.

"Hello to you all. I'm afraid I have some unfortunate news. Professor Handover, my son, will not be joining you all today. He had a heart attack, around 10:00 p.m. Friday night. The alarm was raised by a neighbour who heard a loud crash come from his room, which was caused by the table being knocked over and him hitting the floor. I was told that the ambulance got there quickly, they tried but there was no chance of resuscitation. He had been dead when he hit the floor. Cardiac arrest. They pronounced him dead at the scene at 10:45. He was taken to the morgue, and I was contacted to come and identify the body. There were no suspicious circumstances, the death was by natural causes. They found this piece of paper lying on the floor and gave it to me. I feel that not only is it my duty but it's what he would have wanted, so I will read it to you now."

She unfolded the paper and began:

"My inscription on my tombstone to be read to my dear class of students at the beginning of class twenty. Note to myself, I am so proud of all of them.

"Here lies Professor Handover, mind, body, soul, and heart, which was my least used organ (God, I am so funny). Here's to the journey whenever and however it may end. WE ARE BORN ALONE, AND WE DIE ALONE."

One silent tear rolled down his mother's face.

Class dismissed.

Class Dismissed - A Collection of Epitaphs

The eternal question: how would we all like to be remembered?
Some told a joke, some smiled, a few sang a song. I travelled the
length and breadth of people's psyches to obtain this collection of
tombstone inscriptions.
Ah, if only life (or death) were so simple. It's only words (worth).

Here we go:

SUZI QUATRO   b. 03rd June 1950
    "NOW I GET IT !!!" and on the other side (I am a Gemini
after all)
    "Too many dreams, too little time"

A

ALFRED MARKS   b. 28th January 1921 d. 1st July
1996
    Actor and comedian
    See also Paddy O'Neil (wife)
    "The reason this stone's unnamed and undated,
    is because I am not here,
    I've been cremated"

ALICE COOPER   b. 4th February 1948
    Singer-songwriter and performer
    See also Sheryl Cooper (wife)
    "Here lies Alice and Sheryl Cooper
    from since they were teething

never stopped performing
till they stopped breathing"

ANDY SCOTT   b. 30th June 1949
        Guitarist in Sweet
        "Love is like oxygen
         Too much too high
         Not enough, and then you die"

ARTHUR QUATRO   b. 3rd March 1914   d. 12 October
2008
        "Why should I go to Heaven, I won't know anybody"

B

BOBBY ELLIOTT   b. 9th December 1941
        Drummer in The Hollies
        "Pause and reflect"
        "He could beat a drum, but he couldn't beat this"

BOB GRUEN   b. 23rd October 1945
        Photographer
        "He could have lived a different life but not a better one"

BRIAN MAY   b. 19th July 1942
        Guitarist in Queen
        "Who wants to live forever, when love must die"

BILL KENWRIGHT   b. 4th September 1945   d. 23rd
October 2023
        West End theatre producer and film producer
        "True blue"

BRUCE WELCH   b. 2nd November 1941
        Rhythm guitar for The Shadows
        "To live in hearts we leave behind is not to die"

BRIAN BENNETT   b. 9th February 1940
"If you want to make God laugh, tell him your plans"

C

CHAS HODGES   b. 28th December 1943   d. 22nd
September 2022
Singer, songwriter, vocalist and pianist in Chas and Dave
" Gertcha"

CHERIE CURRIE   b. 30th October 1959
Lead singer in the Runaways, actress
"Your dream is just really waiting to happen"

CLEM CATTINI   b. 20th August 1937
Drummer for the Tornados. Session player for Hermans Hermits, Dusty Springfield, Marianne Faithful, Lou Reed and many more
"Clem Who?" (Look him up, he played on so many hits it's a joke)

CLIFF RICHARD (SIR)   b. 14th October 1940
"Jesus and rock & roll work well together
in the hands of someone who loves them both"

CHRIS MOST   b. 5th January 1942   d. 4th
December 2022
"I did my best"

D

DENIS SELINGER   b. 1921 d. 1991
He was my agent; also agent for Michael Caine and lots of other famous people
"I've always taken 10% of everyone, now they's got 100% of me"

DON POWELL   b. 10th September 1946
      Drummer in Slade
      " You're next"

DENNIS WATERMAN   b. 24th February 1949   d. 8th May
2022
      Actor
      "If there's no sport and no drink, I don't want to go"

DAVID HAMILTON   b. 10th September 1938
      Broadcaster
      "Here lies David Hamilton, stiff at last"

DOROTHY PARKER   b. 22nd August 1893   d. 7th
June 1967
      Poet
      "Excuse my dust"

DAVE MUNDEN   b. 2nd December 1943   d. 2020
      Drummer and singer in the Tremeloes
      "Although resting alone in a box made of wood
      I remember that even my bad times were good"

DEBBIE HARRY   b. 1st July 1945
      Singer for Blondie and actress
      "Farewell"

DONALD DUCK DUNN   b. 24th November 1941   d. 13th
May 2012
      Bass player for Booker T and the MG's amongst others
      "Life's a bitch, then you die"

DAVID ESSEX   b. 23rd July 1947
      "Over and out"

DAVID COURTNEY   b. 17th February 1954   d. 22nd
October 2023
      Author

"I had the time of my life"

E

ERROL BROWN   b. 12th November 1943 d. 6th May 2023

Lead singer of Hot Chocolate
"I started with a kiss, never thought it would come to this"

F

FRANK ALLEN   b. 14th December 1943

Searchers, bass and vox
"Life's amazing tour ended too soon"
"Sex drugs and rock and roll? Not me, I took moderation to excess"

FRANK SCHATZING   b. 28th May 1957

He is an author so has given me a multiple choices; I will use them all.

He is from Germany and very well known around the world
"Not that bad in here"
"You know where to find me"
"Contemplation break"
"That had to happen"
"I knew that was going to happen"

G

GERED MANKOWITZ   b. 3rd August 1946

Photographer
"Dunsnapping"

GRAHAM GOULDMAN   b. 10th May 1946
Singer songwriter, bassist and singer in 10cc
"He played nicely and he shared"

GLYNIS BARBER   b. 25th October 1955
Actress in *Dempsey and Makepeace*
"You remembered to put my phone in, right?"

H

HENRY WINKLER   b. 30th October 1935
"Well King... This case is closed"

HANK MARVIN   b. 28th October 1941
Guitarist with The Shadows
"It's not much of a view, but it's quiet"

HELEN QUATRO   b. 14th February 1914   d. 1992
"You always win with God"

J

JACKIE COLLINS   b. 4th October 1938   d. 19th
September 2015
Author
"She gave a great many people a great deal of pleasure"

JOOLS HOLLAND   b. 24th January 1958
Musician
"Contrary to appearances all is under control"

JENNY SEAGROVE   b. 4th July 1957
Actress
"Excuse me, you're spoiling the view"

JESS CONRAD OBE   b. 24th February 1936
      Actor and singer
      "Here lies Jess Conrad, nobody loved him more than he
loved himself"

JOHN WATSON   b. 4th May 1946
      Winner of five Grand Prix and commentator
      "It would be a waste of life to do nothing with one's ability
      for I feel that life is measured in achievement, not in years
alone"

JOHN McNALLY   b. 30th August 1941
      Searchers
      "Who's closing the show" or
      "I've lived the dream" or
      "What no encore" or
      "You'll never make a living playing that banjo (guitar)
      and that was over 60 years ago"

JOHN LAWS   b. 8th August 1935
      "Goodbye world"

JAY OSMOND   b. 2nd March 1955
      "The best is yet to come"

JOHNNY LOGAN   b. 13 May 1954
      "Hope there's some good music and a decent bar wherever
I'm going…
      Can I have votes from the jury please?"

K

KT TUNSTALL   b. 23 June 1975
      Singer songwriter, musician
      "Jump in, the water's lovely"

KATHY VALENTINE   b. 7th January 1959
        Quoting "Tempus Edam Rerum" - that's all I have, it
means:
        "Time devours everything"

L

LEN TUCKEY   b. 15th December 1945
        Musician (my first husband)
        "Bollocks"

LIONEL JEFFRIES   b. 10th June 1926   d. 19th February
2010
        Actor, director, and screenwriter
        "Here lies Lionel Jeffries, please tell his agent"

LITA FORD   b. 19th September 1958
        Guitar in the Runaways, singer, songwriter
        "Here lies the first lady of rock guitar"

LEO SAYER   b. 21st May 1948
        Singer
        "Have good time, all the time" or
        " Enjoyed everyday with you all while I was here
        but I've even bigger plans when I get upstairs"

LAURA DOYLE   b. 23rd September 1982
        Daughter, singer
        "Thin at last"

LIZ MITCHELL   b. 12 July 1952
        " I lived"

LIAM FIRMAGER   ?
        Director of Suzi Q
        "Died from not forwarding that email to 10 people"

LENNY HENRY (SIR)   b. 29th August 1958
    "Aaaaaaaaaaaaaaand relax" or
    "Press play" or
    "If you can read this you are too bloody close"

LOUIS WALSH   b. 5th August 1952
    "OK he sleeps alone… at last"

LESLIE-ANN JONES   b. 1956
    Author
    "The best book is the next book"

M

MICHAEL CAINE   b. 14th March 1933
    "Been there, done that, and I've got the T-shirt"

MIKE CHAPMAN   b. 13th April 1947
    Songwriter and producer
    "Go away, leave me alone, Why do you think I died?"

MICHAEL WINNER   b. 30th October 1935   d. 21st
January 2013
    Director, producer and restaurant critic
    "Here lies Michael Winner, he will return"

MIKE BATT   b. 6th February 1949
    Singer songwriter, musician, arranger, director, conductor
    "I don't want a fucking tombstone,
    I would like them to flush me down the toilet"

MICK BOX   b. 9th June 1947
    Uriah Heap
    "Happy days and keep rocking"

N

NINA CARTER   b. 4th October 1952
>The Sun page three girl and one of Rik Wakeman's wives
>"As I lie safe and sound,
> I reflect of days gone past
> And leave this note above the ground,
> Thank you for the day off at last.

NINA MYSKOW   b. 18th May 1946
>Journalist
>"Too much was not enough"

P

PADDY O' NEIL   b. 1st May 1926   d. 31st January 2010
>Actress and singer
>See also Alfred Marks (husband)
>"She went unwilling, but in the end, she got top billing"

PAUL O' GRADY   b. 14th June 1955   d. 28th March 2023
>Comedian and presenter
>"At last I can have a nice long lie in"

PALOMA FAITH   b. 21st July 1981
>"Finally, a fucking break"

PAUL GAMBACCINI   b. 2nd April 1949
>"A non moron at number one in Heaven"

R

RULA LENSKA   b. 30th September 1947
   Actress
   "I loved, I laughed, I dreamed, I cried, I've lived my life but now I've died"

RIK WAKEMAN   b. 18th May 1949
   Musician, singer-songwriter, producer and presenter
   "One life is not enough, see you all somewhere else"

RON MOODY   b. 8th January 1924   d. 11th June 2015
   Actor, singer and composer
   "But I haven't started yet"

RICK WESTWOOD ·   b. 7th May 1943
   Guitarist and vocalist in the Tremeloes
   "Here lies the worst singer in the world
   who managed to sing lead on a gold disc, million selling number one record"

RAINER HAAS   b. 3rd March 1945
   Husband and concert promoter
   "I turned left, but it was right"

ROMERO BRITTO   b. 6th October 1963
   Very famous artist who did cover of *Through My Eyes*.
   I have the original picture above my piano in my home.
   "The artist in search of love and happiness"

RICHARD TUCKEY   b. 14th October 1984
   Son and musician.
   "Wait... What?"

ROBBY ROBINSON   b. ???
   "The Lord was his shepherd, the gospel his rhyme,
      Just too much music, just too little time,
      This world is now better because of his songs,
      Robby is missed but where he belongs"

RON HOWARD   b. 1st March 1954
   "Family man and life long story teller."

S

SHERIDAN MORLEY   b. 5th December 1941   d. 16th
February 2007
      Writer and director, his dad was a famous director
      "Here lies a journalist"

STEVE CROPPER   b. 21st October 1941
      Guitarist, songwriter, producer, Booker T and MG's
fabulous player
      Wrote 'Knock on wood'
      "I hope you are ready for this"

SHERYL COOPER   b. 20th May 1956
      See also Alice Cooper (husband)
      "Here lies Alice and Sheryl Cooper,
      from since they were teething,
      never stopped performing
      till they stopped breathing"

T

TIM RICE   b. 10th November 1944
      Lyricist and author
      "I'd rather be under Linda Lusardi"

TERRY UTTLEY   b. 1951 d. 2021
   Bassist in Smokie
   "Always smile and smell good"

V

VICTORY TISCHLER-BLUE b. 16th September 1959
   Vicki Blue, bassist in the Runaways, director and producer
   "Wind blows, rain falls, fire burns…"

Suzi Quatro

Suzi Quatro was born in Detroit, Michigan in 1950. She was raised in a musical family, including three sisters and one brother, who all played various instruments. Suzi made her debut on stage playing bongo's in her fathers jazz band, The Art Quatro Trio. At the age of 14 she started an all girl band with her elder sister Patti, called The Pleasure Seekers. Suzi was 'told' she would be playing bass guitar, which was as tall as her. She quickly became the lead singer and front person. Some years later music producer, Mickie Most, came to a concert and offered Suzi a solo contract. She flew to the UK in 1971 to begin her journey to fame.

In addition to her rock icon fame, Suzi Quatro has written several books. This is the second fiction. She also wrote The Hurricane, released in 2017. She has also 4 large full colour hard cover coffee table books with a selection of poems and lyrics titled; Through My Eyes, Through My Heart, Through My Words and Through My Thoughts.

Suzi Quatro is still a full time working musician and author.

www.ingramcontent.com/pod-product-compliance
Lightning Source LLC
Chambersburg PA
CBHW051137020726
47501CB00005B/1550